Friendship Unveiled

Revealing the True Power of Friendship

John Russell

HoJoPress Publications

To my wife Holli, who has been my most profound inspiration
I love you so much.

Preface

In life's journey, we often find ourselves at a crossroads where our paths intersect with those of others. These moments of connection and camaraderie, forged by the ties of friendship, can become the guiding stars that illuminate our way. "Friendships Unveiled" is an extraordinary journey—a chronicle of how bonds can shape destinies and how searching for truth can lead to profound personal growth.

This book delves into the lives of remarkable individuals who discovered the power of their convictions and the strength of standing together. Holli, Rebeccah, Breanna, Samantha, and others you will meet along the way are united by their unwavering commitment to compassion and the shared pursuit of making the world a better place.

Within these pages, you will find a testament to the resilience of friendship, the transformative potential of unity, and the boundless capacity of the human spirit to evolve and adapt. Through the highs and lows, the laughter and tears, these individuals illustrate the extraordinary growth that can arise when we journey together.

As you immerse yourself in their world, remember that your path may intersect with others when you least expect it, leading to a transformative friendship that shapes the person you are destined to become. In their story, you may find echoes of your own, and in their friendship, you may discover the strength to face your challenges and unveil the infinite possibilities that lie ahead.

Contents

Chapter 1

The California sun painted Sunnyville in golden hues as evening approached. Examining my reflection in the mirror, I embraced my 5-4 stature. I styled my midnight-black hair into cascading waves, framing my face alluringly. My deep, mesmerizing blue-green eyes stared back at me.

Anxious excitement pulsed through me. The punctual version of myself was running late for the charity event—a rarity for someone on time. The need to be ready quickly was evident. Nerves tightened. Realizing this could be a career-changing night, securing a place as a partner at Winston & Associates, a prestigious law firm.

Nestled along the northern California coast, my home graces a lush area. I'm surrounded by vibrant flora, and through the expansive windows, I have breathtaking views of the majestic mountains and the vast stretch of the Pacific Ocean. The soothing melodies of classical music create a tranquil backdrop that resonates throughout the spacious rooms.

Fresh flowers adorned every corner, their delicate fragrance enhancing the luxurious atmosphere of the room. Inhaling, I take in the sweet scent, trying to ease my nerves and channel my focus towards the exciting possibilities of the night.

Slipping into a sleek navy blue dress created a balance of sophistication and allure. The deep hue accentuated my figure and drew attention to my slender waist and shapely legs. The dress complemented my eyes, causing them to shimmer more intensely.

The night had the potential to impact the community. I was excited when I was invited to attend and participate in something bigger than myself. The non-profit Youth Sports and Education Alliance's mission resonated with me. They aimed to raise funds to build football fields for underserved children and the local high school. Contributing to something impactful fueled my desire to be on time.

Looking once more in the mirror, I was grateful for the chance to be a part of something meaningful.

The drive into town was breathtaking. Navigating scenic coastal roads in northern California, lush surroundings painted a picturesque landscape. Tall trees embraced the winding road, and bursts of wildflowers dotted the verges.

The setting sun bathed everything in a warm, golden glow, casting a magical aura. The gentle hum of the engine and distant crashing waves reminded me of the majestic Pacific Ocean beyond the hills. The refreshing scent of salty sea air wafted through my open window, mingling with the earthy fragrance of surrounding forests.

Approaching Harmony Heights, glimmering lights and murmurs greeted me. Smooth traffic resulted from meticulous event planning, allowing for effortless parking. I couldn't resist a glance at the valet area, bustling with luxury vehicles from high-profile attendees. Stepping out, I savored a moment appreciating Harmony Heights.

Perched on a cliff overlooking the ocean, it seamlessly blended modern architecture with nature. The sun setting over the horizon enhanced the magical atmosphere, with fairy lights twinkling on the venue's exterior.

Entering the venue, a live jazz band's soft notes set the tone for the elegant night. The interior was stunning, with tasteful décor that exuded sophistication. Crystal chandeliers cast a warm glow over the marble floors, while plush furnishings were comfortable seating areas for people to mingle.

The air carried the aroma of delectable hors d'oeuvres and gourmet dishes, making my mouth water in anticipation. Servers in crisp white shirts with a subtle sheen tailored to perfection presented a refined appearance. Dark navy blue vests embroidered with the venue's logo in gold thread added a touch of luxury, underlining the occasion. Gliding through the crowd, they offered trays of culinary delights for every palate. The mingling scents of savory and sweet treats heightened the night's ambiance.

Emotions filled the room as guests mingled, united by a common cause. It was evident that everyone present was committed to making a difference in the lives of underserved children. I was part of a collective effort to build football fields for children and support the local high school. Tonight was more than just a professional endeavor; it became a meaningful contribution to the community and a source of inspiration for change.

My gaze swept across the gathering, and I was relieved when I spotted Christopher Blackmon, a colleague of mine. He was a tall man with sandy brown hair that fell over his forehead and could put anyone at ease. His presence was a welcome sight. Our smiles met like old friends reuniting, and we exchanged greetings.

"It's such a pleasant surprise! Didn't expect you to be here tonight, "I exclaimed, my smile reflecting my delight.

Christopher's eyes lit up. "Wouldn't miss this. You look stunning, by the way."

Blushing at the compliment, I replied, "Thank you. You clean up pretty well yourself."

We laughed while catching up on each other's lives and discussing recent events. Sharing anecdotes that carried the easy familiarity of old friends reconnecting. We continued to laugh, catching up on life's twists and turns and exchanging work stories.

Christopher found a former client he wanted to check up on and excused himself. Just then, Senior Partner Brent Nelson walked up to join me. His reputation preceded him. He was a man leading a company that balanced courage and forthrightness. Our paths had crossed, collaborating on campaigns that demanded legal discernment beyond the ordinary. Appreciating Brent's meticulous approach and deep respect for ethical considerations during these ventures.

"Hey, Holli! You are here!" Brent said, extending his hand for a firm handshake.

"Thanks! I was running a bit late," I replied with a hint of sheepishness.

"The important thing is that you're here," he reassured me. By the way, congratulations on handling your last case. The partners were impressed with how you resolved it."

I was proud of his words. "Thank you! It was challenging, but I'm happy it all worked out."

"Of course, you have a knack for tackling the toughest cases," he said, nodding. "That's why everyone respects you at the firm."

Chuckling. "Well, I just try to do my best and bring some charm to the courtroom," I said with a playful wink.

Brent laughed and raised his glass. "To charm and success!"

"To charm and success!" I echoed, clinking my glass with his.

I mingled around the room, I spotted a few familiar faces. I neared Amanda, an arresting woman in her late twenties, gracing a statuesque 5'7". Her long, chestnut-brown hair flowed loosely down her back, elegantly framing her heart-shaped face. She was a Legal Research Assistant at Winston and Associates.

"Hey, Holli!" Amanda said with a smile.

"Hello. Isn't this fantastic?" I replied.

She nodded in agreement. "The rumors are you had a big role in making tonight happen. Kudos to you!"

I blushed, a sense of pride in my involvement. "Well, it was a team effort, but I'm glad to contribute."

Our conversation flowed, and amid it, I couldn't help but notice Mark Fields, the esteemed senior partner —an expert in real estate law. At 6'2", he stood tall, exuding confidence and authority. His athletic build and short, dark brown hair added to his commanding presence, giving him a polished look. A well-maintained beard offered a hint of rugged appeal to his handsome features. His piercing blue eyes held a captivating intensity, mirroring his determination and ambition. Excusing myself, I made my way over to him.

"Good evening, Mark!" I said, extending my hand.

"Hello, Holli! It is an impressive for a wonderful cause," he replied. You and your team did an excellent job. I'm proud to have you as part of our firm."

The compliment from such a respected figure meant a lot to me. "Thank you. I strive to represent the firm's values in everything I do."

We laughed and shared office anecdotes before he encouraged me to continue mingling. Inspired, I moved through the crowd and conversed with others. Laughter and joy filled the air. We all mingled and discussed our enthusiasm for the Youth Sports and Education Alliance; the emotions in the room were contagious.

My nerves subsided as I walked around the room, conversing with various individuals. The elegant backdrop and the interactions with familiar people put me at ease. I was enjoying myself.

I spotted him across the room, and my curiosity got the better of me. I went over to Justin Ford, the famous wide receiver for the Emerald City Thunderhawks. I approached, and he turned to face me, his bright green eyes locking with mine.

"Good evening, Justin. I'm Holli," I said with a warm smile.

"Hello, Holli," he replied, offering his hand for a handshake. "I've seen you at Winston & Associates. People tell me you are the one who is taking care of my contracts. People have said things about your work."

"Oh? I hope it's all good," I said with a hint of playfulness.

He chuckled, his easygoing nature putting me at ease. "You've got quite the reputation for getting things done correctly."

I blushed at the compliment, appreciating the recognition of my professional accomplishments. "Thank you. It's always a joy when people appreciate your work."

"Yeah, and with your contract work, we hope to make a real impact in Sunnyvale with the field and the high school stadium," commented Justin

I've read much about your journey to becoming a pro football player. It's impressive."

A warm smile spread across Justin's face. "Thank you. It's been a wild ride, but I wouldn't have it any other way. Football's been my passion since I was a kid, and now being able to play at this level—it's a dream come true."

"I can imagine. You must have put in a lot of hard work and dedication," I said, intrigued.

"It takes sacrifices, but when you love the game, it's all worth it," he nodded.

We continued talking, I couldn't help but realize the energy and enthusiasm that radiated from him whenever he spoke about football. He had ingrained the sport into his life.

"That's inspiring," I said, meaning it. "It's incredible to witness someone pursue their passion with determination."

Justin's eyes lit up, appreciating the compliment. "Thanks, Holli. What about you? You're a contract attorney. That has to be fascinating."

"It is, and it is fulfilling work," I replied with a sense of pride in my voice.

"So a courtroom is probably like your version of being on the football field," he said with a playful grin.

I laughed. "You could say that. The stakes are high, and a rush of adrenaline when arguing your case. It's also about helping people and making a difference."

"That's awesome," he said, impressed. "It's encouraging to know people like you are fighting for what's right."

I found myself enjoying Justin's company. He was charming and easy to talk to, and I appreciated his genuine interest in my career.

"I have to admit, I'm more of a sports enthusiast than an athlete," I admitted with a grin.

Justin laughed, understanding what I meant. "It's not for everyone. Football's my life, but it's not everyone's cup of tea."

"You must be living every young football player's dream," I said, acknowledging his accomplishments.

"It's been an incredible journey," he smiled. "Enough about me. I'm curious about your work. How did you end up in contract law?"

I enjoyed Justin's company even more as we delved into more personal conversations. Despite being a high-profile professional athlete, he remained down-to-earth and interested in learning about others. Fame hadn't changed him, and I appreciated that.

During our conversation, I admired his curiosity and knack for connecting with people. His genuine interest in beyond the surface made me at ease. I enjoyed our interaction. I felt a mutual attraction, although I recognized that pursuing anything but a friendship with Justin wouldn't align with my lifestyle. My work at Winston & Associates and dedication to important causes were top priorities, and I couldn't afford a relationship that might compromise my focus.

I knew we would remain friends, caution became my guide in involvement without full commitment. Observing its toll on colleagues' lives instilled a determination in me to avoid such pitfalls. Deep within, I acknowledged a craving for a more profound connection—with someone understanding the complexities of the life I held dear.

Among the guests, I was drawn to a flash of vibrant red curls that drew my attention to the woman they adorned. The woman had an energy and charisma that mesmerized everyone around her.

Navigating through the crowd, I was pulled as if the universe conspired to bring us together. Our eyes met, and a connection was forged, binding us like magnets drawn to one another.

"Hi," I greeted her.

Rebeccah's emerald eyes sparkled with enthusiasm. "Hello! I don't believe we've met before. I am Rebeccah Donaldson."

"I'm Holli Bachman," extending my hand, "It's a pleasure to meet you."

"Pleasure to meet you, Holli," Rebeccah commented. "What brings you here tonight?"

"I'm a contract attorney for Winston & Associates and support the charity. We are responsible for all the Youth Sports and Education Alliance contracts. What brings you here tonight?"

Her firm handshake conveyed strength and grace. Sensing a kindred spirit in her magnetic presence. "My team was responsible for promoting and raising awareness about tonight's initiatives and events. My work for tonight was the marketing channels, such as social media, press releases, and influencer partnerships."

I grinned as I admired Rebeccah's stylish attire. "Rebeccah, I must admit, you folks always have the best wardrobe. You all look like you stepped out of a fashion magazine."

"Well, Holli, you lawyers have your sharp suits and power ties, but it's hard to beat the creativity of the marketing world. We can play with colors, patterns, and bold designs." She chuckled, her eyes sparkling with mischief.

"True, but have you ever tried cross-examining a witness in high heels? It's a skill, let me tell you," I said as I raised an eyebrow, feigning a thoughtful expression.

Rebeccah laughed, shaking her head. "I'll give you that one, Holli. I can't imagine chasing after a witness in stilettos. At least you lawyers carry those fancy briefcases. It's like your version of a designer handbag."

In return, a chuckle escaped me. "Ah, yes, the almighty briefcase—a lawyer's best friend. I must admit, I envy your events. They always like a party, whereas our legal gatherings tend to be more formal."

"Well, Holli, maybe one day we'll swap roles. You can navigate the marketing world, and I'll take on the courtroom drama. Just imagine me cross-examining a witness in high heels!" Rebeccah grinned.

I burst into laughter. "Deal! It will be interesting who survives the switch."

We discussed our careers and passions. Rebeccah's passion for creating impactful campaigns was evident in every word she spoke. I shared stories of my experiences as a contract lawyer and how I used charm and personality to help resolve the most challenging cases.

We laughed together, finding common ground in our values of using our positions to make a difference and give back to the community. We delved into more profound subjects, such as our aspirations and dreams, and it was refreshing to connect with someone who understood the importance of making change beyond professional success.

Rebeccah's company was comforting and easy as if we had been friends for much longer than tonight. Her energy was infectious.

Rebeccah began to speak, her eyes gleaming with enthusiasm, "Marketing may not have the same seriousness as law, but it holds its own power. It's about connecting people, shaping perceptions, and inspiring change on a massive scale." Her voice resonated with passion as she spoke about her field.

"We can touch hearts and minds and rally communities. It's a privilege to influence public perception and advocate for causes that can significantly impact people's lives." Rebeccah's words conveyed the depth of her belief in the importance of her work and its potential for creating a better world.

Drawn together as the night progressed, like magnets. Laughter echoed as we shared jokes, discovering we had a similar sense of humor. Exchanging past stories, Rebeccah talked about capturing the marketing bug post-college. Her goal was to connect people, shape perceptions, and have an influence on a massive scale, and she excelled.

"Holli," she began, her voice filled with enthusiasm, "let me tell you about the 'Sports for All.' It was a significant change for everyone involved."

Rebeccah's smile radiated as she recounted the campaign's accomplishments. "Our goal was to promote inclusivity and provide underprivileged children access to athletic programs. We crafted a message that touched people's hearts across the country. It was all about breaking down barriers and ensuring that every child, regardless of their background, had the chance to play and be part of a team."

She leaned forward, her eyes shining with passion. "The response was incredible! It wasn't just about the number of likes or shares on social media but about real change."

Rebeccah's enthusiasm was contagious. She continued, "The support was an outpouring from both the public and corporate partners. We partnered with local schools, organized clinics, and provided scholarships for underprivileged children to join teams. It was a movement."

She paused for a moment, her expression filled with emotion. "I remember visiting one of the schools where we had implemented the program. The smiles on the children's faces when they played their first game or scored their first goal were priceless, Holli. That's when I experienced the joy of making a difference."

I listened to Rebeccah's story, admiring my new friend's passion and dedication. With a warm smile, I responded, "That's incredible!"

"I've always believed that our professions can be a significant tool for change," I added. Continuing, "Listening to your story reminds me of the countless ways we can use our skills to create change," I said with conviction. "I began giving back to the community using my legal expertise, which has always been my driving force." I continued, "Over the years, I've taken on numerous pro bono cases to help those in need. A particular case stands out in my memory. Representing a low-income family facing eviction, they were struggling to maintain a roof over their heads, on the brink of losing their home. I poured tireless effort, transforming it from a mere legal matter into something more profound," I shared.

"Understanding their struggles and dreams, their story touched my heart. I was resolute in fighting for their rights, ensuring a fair chance for them to stay in their home." With a soft smile, I continued, "It's moments like those reaffirm my commitment to using my skills for the greater good. The satisfaction I gain from helping others who wouldn't have had access to representation is immeasurable." I leaned back, reflecting on even the more minor acts of service.

Rebeccah nodded in agreement, her fiery red hair gleaming in the soft glow of the lights. "It's not just about climbing the ladder; it's about extending a hand to those who need it."

We exchanged contact information. Rebeccah handed me her business card with a mischievous grin. "Call me anytime, Holli. We're going to do some amazing things together."

Tucking the card into my clutch, a sense of anticipation for the adventures that lay ahead enveloped me. "I can't wait," came my reply, filled with genuine enthusiasm.

The venue still buzzed with energy. The sights and sounds of the night lingered in the air, creating a magical ambiance that seemed to wrap around me. The soft glow of elegant chandeliers cast a warm and inviting light, illuminating the laughter and smiles of the guests as they mingled and bid their farewells.

The connection I had forged with Rebeccah assured me of a future filled with meaningful collaborations. It held the potential to make a real difference in the community.

Leaving the venue, I stepped out into the cool night air of Sunnyville. The city's lights glittered in the distance, and the soft, gentle breeze carried the scent of salt from the nearby Pacific Ocean. Walking to my car, I caught glimpses of others departing, their faces reflecting a sense of fulfillment and inspiration.

The evening exceeded my expectations. Meeting Rebeccah had been an unexpected blessing. Our conversation tonight was more than just a casual exchange. It began a friendship built on values and aspirations.

Navigating Sunnyville's winding roads, I pondered about the people I met and the exchange with Rebeccah. I smiled while parking my car in the driveway. The serendipitous encounter with Rebeccah unveiled possibilities, eager to experience where this partnership would lead. I stepped into my home, ready to embrace the bright future ahead.

Chapter 2

The curtains fluttered in the morning breeze. The sun's golden rays kissed my face, coaxing me awake and casting a warm glow across the room. Fresh coffee wafted through the air, inviting me to start the day on a rejuvenating note. I got out of bed. The soft carpet underfoot comforted me, preparing me for the day ahead.

My fingers danced across the bathroom tiles, skillfully adjusting the taps for the perfect hot and cold water balance. Steam enveloped me as the ritualistic shower refreshed my senses. Citrus-scented body wash left an invigorating aroma. Dressed in a crisp, professional black suit radiating confidence and charm, I gazed at the panoramic cityscape beyond the window. The bustling tapestry of buildings reached for the sky while the world below hummed with life. The sight filled me with anticipation for the day's activities.

Despite being known for my punctuality and dedication to being on time, the memory of the charity event flashed through my mind. The memory rushed back like a whirlwind. I saw the spilled champagne, the hurried apologies, and the amused glances of the other guests as I arrived late. That rare occurrence reminded me to stay prepared for unforeseen circumstances and allowed me to approach the day with both readiness and flexibility.

I made my way to my car. The sound of chirping birds and the gentle rustling of leaves in the breeze filled the air with the symphony of nature awakening to the day. The aroma of blooming flowers greeted me as I stepped outside, and the early morning sunshine cast a golden hue over the neighborhood.

Driving to Winston and Associates, the city was already bustling with activity. The morning commute was in full swing, with cars filling the streets. The parking lot at the firm was abuzz with activity as well, but to my relief, ample spots were still available for me to park my car.

Stepping from the car, the morning sun wrapped me in warmth, a quick moment of solar solace. It was a gentle embrace, a pick-me-up for the day. With confidence, I strode to Winston and Associates' entrance. The glass doors parted, and I stepped onto the polished marble floors. Natural light flooded through the windows, casting a radiant glow. The foyer is calm yet bustling, and employees complete their morning tasks.

The hum of activity greeted me as I stepped into the grand lobby of Winston and Associates. The sound of ringing phones, the hushed conversations among colleagues, and the occasional tap of heels created a professional yet bustling atmosphere.

Navigating the entrance, my eyes scanned the room, absorbing the familiar surroundings. She caught my attention there—April Fague, the Youth Sports and Education Alliance's Programs Coordinator. In her late twenties, she stood by the reception desk, exuding a warm and approachable aura while conversing with one of the firm's partners. April looked radiant in a taupe dress that complemented her bright blonde hair; her warm smile echoed her deep passion for impactful work.

I hesitated, unsure if she'd recognize me. It's been a while since we last met at the charity event, but her magnetic personality and passion for the cause are unforgettable. Taking a deep breath, I walked up to her, hoping she'd remember our conversation from that memorable night.

I approached April glanced in my direction, and her eyes lit up with recognition. "Holli, right?" she said, her voice filled with genuine warmth.

"Yes," I replied, relieved that she remembered. "It's great to see you again, April. You're doing a fantastic job with the Youth Sports and Education Alliance."

Her smile widened, and she nodded. "Thank you, Holli. Your support at the charity event meant a lot to all of us. We couldn't have done it without Winston and Associates' help."

"It was our pleasure to be a part of such a meaningful cause," I said, meaning every word. April and I walked to the elevator and got in. Amidst the brief silence of the elevator ride, I couldn't help but notice April standing beside me. Her vibrant energy was infectious.

The elevator doors opened as we reached the designated floor and entered the bustling hallway. April greeted everyone we passed with genuine warmth and kindness. She was well-liked and respected by everyone at the firm, and I could understand why. Her passion for empowering young minds through sports and education shone through in every interaction she had.

Making our way toward my office, April continued to engage in pleasantries with various colleagues and team members. She had a way of making each interaction feel personal and meaningful, impacting everyone she encountered. We reached my office, and April paused to discuss the contract for the high school stadium. "Holli, I just wanted to thank you again for your assistance with the contract. Your expertise and attention to detail have been invaluable," expressing gratitude.

"It was my pleasure. I'm glad I could contribute to such a meaningful project," I replied, appreciating her acknowledgment.

April continued, "I've reviewed the terms, and they are comprehensive. I'll have it finalized by the end of the day."

I smiled, pleased with the progress. "Thank you! Your dedication is inspiring, and I'm glad to have played a part in it. I'll review the contract and get back to you if there are any further details to discuss."

April bid me farewell and continued toward Mark's office to discuss the real estate contracts for the youth football fields. I settled into my office and felt satisfied, knowing that my work had contributed to something greater than myself.

The morning light filtered through the large windows, casting a warm and welcoming glow over my workspace. The soft hum of activity filled the air as colleagues went about their tasks, each immersed in their responsibilities. The familiar sounds of clicking keyboards, hushed conversations, and ringing phones created a harmonious symphony of productivity.

I took a moment to appreciate the view from my window—a stunning panorama of the city stretching out before me. Tall buildings stood like sentinels, reaching for the sky while pedestrians and vehicles filled the bustling streets below. The city's energy was infectious and fueled my determination to tackle the contracts awaiting my attention.

Near the water cooler, a group erupted in laughter. Their jokes and banter were a testament to the strong sense of community that valued cooperation and teamwork. I focused on the contracts, and the bursts of laughter echoed, bringing a smile to my face. The contagious positivity in the air made the contract review feel less daunting.

Noon approached, and lunch filled the air, permeating the office space and tempting my taste buds. The soft shuffle of footsteps echoed in the hallway as colleagues approached the break room or to leave for nearby eateries. The enticing aroma of various cuisines mingled, creating a compelling symphony distracting me from the task at hand.

I took in the mouthwatering scents, I realized that I had planned to meet Rebeccah for lunch today. I anticipated catching up with my newfound friend. Glancing at the clock, I confirmed it was time for our lunch appointment. Gathering my belongings, I navigated the busy sidewalks. I moved toward the restaurant where Rebeccah and I were to meet. Despite my demanding schedule and the gravity of my work, the anticipation of our upcoming lunch made me smile. These moments of friendship and connection were cherished, balancing the intensity of my professional life.

Arriving at the restaurant, I spotted Rebeccah sitting at a cozy corner table, her vibrant red curls standing out in the natural light that filtered through the windows. She looked as radiant as ever, her smile lighting up the room as our eyes met.

I sat across from Rebeccah and engaged in light-hearted small talk, catching up on recent events and sharing anecdotes about our day-to-day lives. The atmosphere was relaxed, and her magnetic presence made it easy for the conversation to flow.

"So, how's work been treating you?" I asked, taking a sip of my drink.

Rebeccah grinned, her eyes sparkling with enthusiasm. "Oh, you know how it is in the world of marketing. There is always something exciting happening! We just wrapped up a successful campaign for another local charity, and the response has been overwhelming."

"That sounds amazing!" I complimented.

During our lunch, I could tell something weighed on Rebeccah's mind. Engaging in light small talk, I saw her struggling to find the right words. With a deep breath, she began, "Holli, something is troubling me that I need to share with you. I stumbled upon some disturbing information while working on a marketing campaign."

I set my fork down, my curiosity piqued. "Disturbing information? What do you mean?"

She hesitated before continuing, "The company I work for may be engaging in exploitative labor practices. "Behind their crafted public image may be a darker reality."

Her words intrigued me. I asked, "What kind of information did you uncover?"

She inhaled, and her eyes bore the weight of the information she carried. "It all began with a minor discrepancy in some supplier details," she recounted. "I decided to delve deeper, and what unfolded before me was unsettling. In the remote corners of Southeast Asia, a supplier is touted as the source for a clothing line marketing as 'eco-friendly' and 'ethically produced.' I cross-referenced this data with reports from non-governmental organizations (NGOs) dedicated to scrutinizing labor practices in the region. The truth is becoming more evident with every layer I am peeling back. The supplier, it appears, has a shadowy history with labor violations, including child labor, sub-poverty wages, and dangerous working conditions."

Rebeccah exhaled. "It surprises me, but they work with several clients in the fashion and electronics industries. These clients outsource their production to other countries to cut costs, and that's where the issue arises."

Curiosity piqued, I leaned in, wanting to grasp the complete picture. "So, you're saying that the exploitative practices are happening within the supply chains of the company's clients?"

Rebeccah nodded. "The company I'm working with is in charge of marketing and promoting the products of these clients. We create advertisement campaigns highlighting the benefits of the products and their clients' positive image while, behind the scenes, these unethical practices riddle the manufacturing process. EthicalEdge presents a positive and desirable image of the products, misleading consumers about how these products were made could jeopardize our reputation."

Nodding, I said, absorbing the information. "So, does the company contribute to the exploitation by promoting these products without revealing the truth about their production?"

Rebeccah nodded. "Yes, that's it. The more successful they are at marketing these products, the more demand there is, which means the manufacturers encourage cutting corners even more, leading to further exploitation. We could be helping these companies make money and exploit people, especially children."

The severity of the situation weighed on both of us. It was evident that Rebeccah had discovered something that demanded action, and I knew that standing by her side meant taking on a responsibility beyond usual marketing duties. The path ahead was uncertain, but I wanted to support Rebeccah in ensuring that the truth about these exploitative practices became exposed.

The gravity of the situation was sinking in, and I could understand why Rebeccah was so troubled by this discovery. Exploiting workers in such a way was wrong and illegal. Knowing that speaking out could jeopardize her career, I could see how much this affected her.

"This is a lot to take in," I said, trying to be supportive.

Rebeccah nodded. "I know. I couldn't stay silent about it. The public should know the truth. Especially if there are unethical practices involving children. I've been digging into this for some time now, and it's not an isolated issue. It's a pervasive problem, touching various industries, such as garment manufacturing, electronics, and agriculture. These practices thrive in countries where labor laws are nonexistent, and the workers have no voice. It's not just about grueling hours; it's about meager wages, hazardous conditions, and blatant human rights violations."

My brow furrowed as I grappled with the enormity of her words. "This is more extensive than I ever imagined. The company you're working for, they're implicated in all of this?"

Rebeccah nodded, the weight of truth evident in her gaze. "Yes, they market these products while obscuring the harsh realities behind their production. It's all about profits to them, and they ignore the suffering of these workers."

Drawing closer, my determination grew more assertive. "We need concrete evidence, Rebeccah, but we must also brace ourselves for potential repercussions. Powerful interests may attempt to keep this hidden."

A steely resolve came over Rebeccah's face. "I know."

We continued our lunch, our conversation centered on the difficult path ahead. We discussed the importance of collecting concrete evidence and how to approach the matter without jeopardizing our careers. It was clear that Rebeccah was determined to make a difference, and I was there to support her.

We finished our meal, and a sense of urgency crept over us. The weighty conversation still hung in the air. Our eyes met in a shared moment of understanding, a silent agreement passing between us. It was as if our thoughts converged, and we acknowledged the gravity of the situation, our minds racing with the seriousness of the information we had uncovered. We couldn't afford to let this ethical dilemma linger.

Determined, I reached out and placed my hand over Rebeccah's, offering a supportive squeeze. "Thank you for sharing this with me," I said.

She nodded, her eyes reflecting concern, fear, and resolve. "I'm glad I have you by my side, Holli. Your support means a lot to me."

We stood up to leave, taking a moment to embrace each other, finding comfort in our friendship.

"We should schedule a meeting for Saturday to review the evidence and strategize," Rebeccah proposed, her voice exuding determination. "Our approach needs to be meticulous and calculated. , I'd like to enlist the help of a few of my friends for this endeavor."

"Agreed," I replied, feeling a sense of responsibility settle on my shoulders. "We'll gather all the information and decide the best course of action."

Outside, the sun bathed the city, casting long shadows as people hurried by. We parted ways, I felt mixed emotions—apprehension about the challenges ahead and a sense of hope.

Chapter 3

I t was early Saturday morning. A breeze created a soothing melody, complemented by the distant chirping of birds, their cheerful tunes adding to the serene atmosphere. The view from my porch was a sight. Lush greenery adorned my backyard, with colorful flowers in full bloom.

The sun's soft rays bathed everything in a warm, golden glow, casting long shadows across the lawn. Dewdrops sparkled like diamonds on the blades of grass, and a subtle mist hovered above the ground, giving the surroundings an ethereal touch. The air was crisp and fresh, carrying the faint scent of earth and blooming flowers, invigorating my senses and preparing me for the day ahead.

I wore a light, flowing white blouse and comfortable dark jeans, and my hair was pulled back into a neat ponytail, a relaxed yet put-together look. I took a moment to breathe in the calming ambiance, letting my back porch's sights and sounds envelop me in peace. The world slowed down, allowing me to appreciate the beauty of the present.

Invigorated by my coffee, I headed to my car. The smooth drive to Rebeccah's house flowed, and the traffic maintained a light pace. The city presented quieter streets compared to its usual weekday hustle. The engine guided me through familiar roads, passing charming neighborhoods and well-kept gardens. The city's blend of modern and historic architecture added a unique touch. Amid the occasional jogger and dog walker, I embraced the cool morning breeze.

The surroundings transformed as I neared Rebeccah's neighborhood. Towering trees bordered the streets, their branches weaving a verdant tapestry overhead. The area emitted a warm and inviting aura adorned with tended lawns and amiable neighbors who exchanged waves as I passed by.

The earlier view from my back porch had felt like the calm preceding a storm. I quickened my pace, revealing my heightened enthusiasm. I stood at Rebeccah's front door, anticipation coursed through my veins. The door opened, and Rebeccah's smile spread across her face as she greeted me. Her vibrant red curls cascaded down her shoulders, framing her beaming expression.

She wore a simple yet stylish knee-length sundress with a floral pattern that complemented her radiant personality. Her outfit choice reflected the casual comfort of the weekend, which matched her home's peaceful ambiance.

The scene that met my eyes exuded a comforting and hospitable atmosphere as she welcomed me indoors. Our embrace conveyed the reunion of dear friends who had not seen each other in far too long. Rebeccah's home boasted tasteful decor, bathed in soothing earthy hues and punctuated with verdant accents that contributed to the room's inviting atmosphere. Sunlight streamed through the windows, cleaning the space in a gentle, radiant glow.

The air was a mix of scents—the subtle aroma of brewed coffee lingered, mingling with the sweet fragrance of a scented candle on a nearby shelf. The soft whirring of a fan and the occasional rustling of papers added to the homey atmosphere. Sitting with Rebeccah, the ringing doorbell disrupted our peaceful day. Rebeccah rose and headed towards the door. Her friends, Breanna and Samantha, standing on the doorstep. Rebeccah, always one for playful banter, took the opportunity to introduce them in a lighthearted manner.

With a warm smile and a mischievous twinkle in her eye, Rebeccah began, "Allow me to introduce Breanna Willis, our resident fearless investigative reporter, who once attempted to interview a squirrel, and Samantha Williams, our resident hacker extraordinaire, whose laptop boasts more secret identities than a spy thriller character."

We all laughed at Rebeccah's introductions. Rebeccah had informed me about the story of their friendship. They met during a college journalism course, bonding over their passion for injustices. This common interest forged a strong connection between them. Over the years, their friendship continued to thrive, transcending their college days. They remained in close contact, offering each other support in their respective pursuits and arranging meetups whenever their schedules allowed.

Despite their different careers and interests, their friendship remained intact. Breanna became a fearless investigative reporter with a penchant for uncovering the truth. Samantha honed her technical skills to become a talented white hat computer hacker, but no one ever questioned who she worked for or where.

Breanna stood next to me with her fiery red hair falling to her shoulders. She had her signature style of business casual with a hint of boldness. Breanna wore a fitted blazer over a t-shirt, jeans, and ankle boots. Beside her was Samantha. Her blonde hair framed her face, and her mischievous smile hinted at the countless technical feats she had accomplished. She rocked a more laid-back look—a vintage tee, cargo pants with various pockets, and colorful sneakers.

We laughed about the late-night study sessions and the adrenaline-fueled investigative pursuits. The friendship over the years was evident, and I seamlessly joined the college gang. Our conversation unfolded, leading us to a lively recounting of their college pranks and humorous anecdotes.

Rebeccah laughed, "Remember when we pulled that all-nighter to catch a ghost in the library? Turned out to be a janitor in a sheet!"

Breanna said, "Samantha hacked into the university's grading system to give us all 'A+s' for bravery."

Laughter filled the air as the women reminisced about their college days. Rebeccah brought in snacks and drinks as we caught up on each other's lives. Breanna told stories about her latest investigative reports. Samantha recounted her recent hacking adventure for a noble cause. I discussed my legal work and the significant case Rebeccah, and I embarked upon.

We shared our respective journeys, and it became evident that our paths had converged for a purpose. Breanna's investigative skills and Samantha's technical expertise added to our investigative team.

"Why not just go to the authorities?" Samantha asked. It was a valid question, one that we all pondered. Lingering like a challenge, Samantha's question met an uncertain response from Rebeccah.

Rebeccah hesitated before replying, "I don't know if I can trust anyone right now to conduct a thorough and unbiased investigation."

Rebeccah's words settled on us as we realized the enormity of the task ahead. Breanna's voice joined the conversation, expressing her concern about the potential dangers. "I am all for a good investigation, but this may be dangerous," she warned. We can't ignore this exploitation, which impacts children."

Samantha asked, "So what's our plan? Where do we start?" The questions were simple, but we all had limited experience in crime investigation without the authorities' involvement.

Rebeccah added, "I've been researching the company's activities and connections. Our first move should be to gather information. The more information, the better we can strategize."

Settling in, we began discussing our approach. Rebeccah and I took charge of the Research and Documentation, leveraging her familiarity with EthicalEdge Solutions to gather records and documents. My role was to review the information, looking for any discrepancies or areas of concern.

Breanna and Rebecca embraced their roles as the networking and interview duo, a seamless fit given their backgrounds. Breanna's extensive contact list promised a lot of potential interviews—current and former employees, suppliers, and competitors. They poised themselves to gain a comprehensive understanding of the company.

With a sly grin, Breanna quipped, "Alright, team, it's time to play detective with real people. Samantha, no hacking into the coffee machine this time, okay?"

Samantha replied, "I can't make any promises. That coffee machine might have had it coming. It could've been a double agent."

We all laughed. The living room became a makeshift command center as we scrambled to prepare our laptops. Restlessness filled the space. Rebeccah's fingers danced in a rhythmic cadence on her laptop's keyboard, determined to unearth details about EthicalEdge Solutions. Breanna, phone in hand, worked to arrange interviews with her network of contacts. Samantha's nimble fingers danced across her laptop keyboard, embracing her role. Her expertise was a valuable asset.

Samantha announced, "I'm diving into the digital realm. I'll be hunting for online traces, connections, and potential leaks. If there's mischief afoot in cyberspace, I'll be the one to uncover it."

Our voices echoed in the room, exchanging plans and ideas. Occasional laughter blended with the severe tones of our discussions. We agreed to keep each other informed every step of the way. Regular meetings and updates were crucial. We decided to meet at the library next Saturday to compare notes.

The sun began to set, and the evening approached. We bid our farewells in Rebeccah's cozy living room. The warm golden light filtered through the curtains, creating a serene ambiance. The soft glow illuminated our determined and hopeful faces for the task ahead.

Rebeccah's warm smile conveyed her gratitude for her friends' support. "Thank you for being here. Your willingness to help means the world to me."

I spoke up, "Rebeccah. This is important, and I'm proud to be a part of it."

Exiting Rebeccah's house, the evening air greeted us with a gentle embrace, and the subtle scent of blooming flowers wafted through the neighborhood.

Samantha declared, "Hey, if you happen to stumble upon any suspicious cats or rogue toaster ovens online, just know it's probably my handiwork."

I couldn't help but smile as I settled into my car, the bond of friendship forming. Thoughts of the impending investigation swirled in my mind.

I arrived at my porch and took a moment to reflect on the evening. Entering my home, I couldn't help but let out a contented sigh. After a long day of planning and discussions, I needed time to unwind and recharge.

I kicked off my shoes and settled on the couch, putting my feet up. With my eyes closed, I took a moment to let the day's events sink in. I leaned back. The comfort of my familiar surroundings enveloped me.

The soft cushions of the couch provided cozy support, and the gentle hum of my home filled the air. The sounds of distant neighbors and the occasional passing car created a soothing symphony, lulling me into a state of relaxation. The day's events lifted as I closed my eyes, anticipating what may happen tomorrow.

Chapter 4

S itting in the comfort of my cozy kitchen, I savored the homemade sandwich I'd whipped up for lunch. The scent of toasted bread mingled with the tangy aroma of fresh tomatoes, filling the air and making my mouth water. Sunlight streamed through the window, casting a warm glow on the wooden table where I sat, adding a sense of serenity.

The sounds of the neighborhood outside drifted in a distant murmur of passing cars and the occasional laughter of kids playing in the street. The typical hustle and bustle subdued me, allowing for tranquil reflection.

Recollections of yesterday's adventures with my new friends played in my mind. The determination in Breanna's voice, Samantha's tech prowess, and Rebeccah's comforting presence all left a mark on me. Their friendship lingered, even in the stillness of the morning.

Glancing out the window, I saw the gentle sway of the trees in the light breeze. It was a soothing sight that complemented the peacefulness of the moment. The subtle ticking of the clock on the wall added a rhythm to the scene, punctuating the tranquility of the afternoon.

Taking a sip of my coffee, I found a sense of contentment in the simplicity of the meal and the comforting ambiance of my home. Moments like these, away from the rush of the outside world, allowed me to appreciate the joy of a quiet lunch and the fond memories of newfound friendships.

I grabbed my phone, dialing Rebeccah's number. The buzz tingled through my fingers as I waited for her to answer. A few rings later, her cheerful voice filled my ear.

"Rebeccah! How's it going?" I greeted her with a spark of excitement.

"Hey, Holli! I'm good. What's up?" she replied with a friendly warmth.

"I thought we should shake things up today. Do something fun, something different," I suggested, my words tinged with a hint of adventure.

"Ah, I'm up for that! What do you have in mind?" Rebeccah asked, her curiosity evident.

"How about something that challenges us, an escape room?" I proposed.

"That's brilliant! I've been dying to try one of those. I know a place nearby. What do you think?" Rebecca asked.

"Sounds good." I agreed, already noticing the adrenaline rush. "Hey, why don't we grab dinner at that cozy bistro on the corner of Main Street?" I suggested.

"Holli, that's perfect. I'll reserve a table for us to enjoy a good meal," Rebeccah replied.

"Let's get Breanna and Samantha to join us. It'll make for a fantastic girls' night," Rebeccah suggested, her voice bursting with enthusiasm.

After a quick power nap to recharge, I sprang up, refreshed, and ready for the night. I chose a deep purple blouse that made me feel confident and slipped into dark jeans. Comfortable yet stylish- the perfect ensemble for the evening's adventure.

The engine hummed as I navigated through downtown, the city lights painting a colorful tapestry against the evening sky. I steered through the traffic, the rhythmic sound of the turn signal accompanying my journey to the bistro. The streets were alive with activity, people winding down their day, and the honk piercing through the urban symphony. The city's pulse was vibrant, contrasting with the peaceful calm awaiting us.

I stepped out of the car, and the bistro's warm lights embraced us in their golden hue. Rebeccah stood in a chic outfit- a striped blouse paired with jeans - exuding an air of comfort and style. Samantha wore a vintage leather jacket complementing her edgy look. Breanna's business-casual ensemble sported a blazer over a graphic tee.

Emotions swirled- for the evening ahead. The night's escapade, Rebeccah, Samantha, and Brenna's beaming faces mirrored my own.

We entered and followed the hostess to a corner table near the street window. The server, a young woman with a smile, approached us. Her upbeat attitude radiated as she handed us the menus and took our drink orders.

The bistro hummed with a soothing ambiance. Laughter and chatter intertwined, creating a gentle atmosphere. The scent of savory dishes teased my senses. Warm light spilled across the room, glowing on the wooden tables and rustic decor. Customers engaged in animated conversations.

A faint gurgle of a baby's laughter resonated, adding a delightful innocence. Rebeccah's eyes lit up as she waved at a toddler nearby, the child's smiles and gleeful giggles echoing through the room.

Our emotions were high, a sense of eagerness and camaraderie enveloping us. The night's activity sparked excitement among us, reflected in the chatter and the sparkle in our eyes.

The server engaged us in conversation, inquiring about our day. Samantha shared our evening plans, mentioning the Escape Room on 1st Street.

"I've been there," she replied, keeping the details a secret. "It's really cool, and I won't spoil the surprise. Trust me, the ending will catch you off guard. Ever been to one?

"This is my first time," I exclaimed. "I can't wait to go. They're supposed to be a blast. I'm curious. Will you have any hints on how we should handle the clues," I inquired.

She smiled in response, "Now, if I tell you that, it will take away all the fun."

The conversation bubbled for the upcoming event as we looked over the menu. Talk of the evening's adventure seamlessly transitioned into discussions about our families.

"Tonight's going to be fun," Samantha exclaimed, her enthusiasm infectious. "I can't wait to put our heads together and tackle the escape room."

"Yeah, it's going to be amazing," Breanna agreed, her eyes shining. "These challenges bring out my competitive side, but I know we will need to do this together."

Rebeccah nodded, her smile warm and encouraging. "We'll nail it." We wrapped up our delightful dinner. We settled the bill and strolled out of the bistro, eager for the adventure ahead. We headed to the escape room, expectations bubbling with every step.

The building stood tall, adorned with neon signs that lit up the evening. A flashing marquee welcomed us, showcasing the name in vibrant colors.

The lobby hummed with activity. The faint sound of music and buzz from other participants filled the air. The room charged with excitement and fueled us.

We exchanged excited glances as we took in the surroundings, our eagerness palpable. The hope of what lay ahead mingled with the place's electric energy, making the atmosphere crackle with a touch of nervousness.

I approached the counter and paid for our tickets, and tension built up as I handed over the money. The attendant gave them to us with a smile and directed us to the waiting room.

Groups huddled around, discussing strategies and sharing nervous laughs. The reception area showcased posters and murals, showcased previous winners, and teased the challenges inside. Ticking clocks on the wall added a suspenseful touch to the atmosphere.

We entered the room, eager for our turn. The air crackled with nerves, and our eyes gleamed with the impending fun.

The escape room's theme emerged as a mad scientist's lair. The room was shrouded in mystery, with scientific apparatus scattered around, blinking lights, and a dramatic soundtrack in the background. Solving the riddles and puzzles within an hour or "face humiliation" at the end was straightforward. The stakes were high, adding extra tension to the atmosphere.

The room buzzed with energy as we began unraveling the clues, and the air hummed with the concentration of urgency. The puzzles required us to work together, piecing fragmented hints and codes together to unlock the next stage. Each solved puzzle brought us closer to the final solution, but the pressure of the ticking clock added an edge to the night.

Our collective focus was palpable, and the room echoed with our discussions, deliberations, and gasps of realization as we deciphered the clues. It was an exhilarating race against time, the adrenaline driving us forward.

The first clue in the room revolved around a set of laboratory notes left behind. The backstory was that a scientist known for groundbreaking experiments had developed a serum promising enhanced intelligence. The notes detailing the serum's creation were encrypted. Deciphering required decoding a formula inscribed in intricate symbols or a cipher.

The goal was to unveil the key components essential for replicating the serum. Based on the clues scattered throughout the room, we needed to rearrange certain chemicals or elements, each hinting at a part of the formula.

This initial puzzle could involve locating hidden compartments or drawers containing fragmented pieces. The formula would unlock a new room section or provide a code to access the next set of clues.

We huddled around the cryptic notes, the thrill of tonight reflected in our eager expressions. The room pulsed, the air tinged with curiosity.

"Alright, team, let's crack this code," Rebeccah's voice enthusiastically echoed.

Samantha leaned closer, her fingers tracing the intricate patterns. "These symbols connect. It's a pattern we need to follow."

Breanna nodded, her eyes alight with focus. "Agreed. Let's decipher them. There must be a sequence hidden in the cryptic messages."

The air filled with the rustling of papers and the soft murmur of our theories. We all offered insights and suggestions, the gasp signaling a potential breakthrough.

"I think I've found a clue here," I exclaimed.

Rebeccah's eyes widened. "That might be it. Let's piece this together. Our dialogue danced between a collaborative effort driving us deeper. The room became a stage for our shared enthusiasm, the pulsating energy palpable as we solved the enigmatic puzzle.

The room buzzed with intensity. Breanna deciphered a complex code, Samantha unearthed hidden compartments, and Rebeccah pieced the elusive patterns. I connected the dots, and with a triumphant click, the door creaked open.

"The final clue," Samantha exclaimed.

Our victorious laughter filled the room as we stepped out, clocking in at 55 minutes. Pride surged within us, evident in our beaming smiles and the exchange of high fives.

The waiting area outside reverberated with cheers and applause from the staff, congratulating us on our swift escape. Our triumph echoed through the hallway, a testament to our teamwork. The satisfaction of unraveling the puzzle united us, leaving us elated and proud of our accomplishments.

We strolled back, and the playful banter bubbled between us, echoing through the quiet street. Breanna kidded with Samantha about her quick hacking skills. Samantha fired back with a witty remark about Breanna's investigative prowess, and Rebeccah added her trademark humor to the mix. I joined in, ribbing them about their animated reactions.

"Who knew decoding secret messages was in your skill set, Breanna?" Samantha joked.

"Hey, hacking isn't always the answer, Sam," Breanna retorted, earning a round of chuckles.

"I thought the investigative reporter would have all the answers? I teased Breanna, nudging Rebeccah.

"It's called strategizing, Holli," Breanna said with a smirk, feigning seriousness and a playful wink.

Our laughter and teasing carried us to the car, the bond of friendship growing stronger with every jest and chuckle.

We bid our farewells. We hugged, knowing that this escape room was more than just fun: a precursor to the real challenges awaiting us. Our parting words echoed a mutual resolve to unravel the mysteries behind EthicalEdge Solutions.

The drive home was a quiet yet contemplative journey. The city lights flickered against the night sky, casting a serene glow on the streets. I navigated through the familiar roads, and the day's events replayed like a vivid movie. As I pulled into my driveway, I felt fulfilled, knowing we were taking the first steps toward something meaningful.

Chapter 5

The faint scent of printed paper mingled with the aroma of the coffee I had brought from the break room. It was a bittersweet reminder of the long hours I had been putting in. A stack of files lay before me, a testament to the demanding workload defined this week at the law firm.

A phone call from an unexpected source would soon turn this ordinary day into a whirlwind of intrigue. The clock on the wall ticked away, a constant nudge of time slipping through my fingers as I navigated complex cases.

Fatigue tugged at my shoulders, and frustration simmered beneath the surface. Despite my efforts, progress had been slow, and the mounting pressure threatened to erode my resolve. There were moments when I wanted to give up, and the thought of escaping my profession's relentless demands seemed almost tempting. The exhaustion was evident. My eyes, weary from hours of scrutinizing legal documents, as I rubbed my temples. The clattering of keyboards and the distant echoes of hushed conversations blended into a dissonant symphony.

The essence of my profession lay in navigating uncharted territories and overcoming obstacles. Clenching the armrests of my chair, my spine rigid, I drew in a slow, steadying breath. The desire to give in loomed like a shadow, but I forced it into the recesses of my thoughts. The office's familiar sights and sounds, which had been a backdrop to triumphs and tribulations, held a silent promise of resilience as I returned to the files. A sense of quiet resolve settled within me.

My phone's muted ringtone broke the concentration engulfed me in the office. Glancing at the caller's ID, I recognized the number belonging to a client I assisted. With a quick inhale to compose myself, I answered the call.

"Hello, this is Holli Bachman."

The voice on the other end sounded relieved but hurried. "Hi, Holli, it's Dawn Riley. I hope I'm not catching you at a bad time."

"Not at all. I'm here to help. What can I do for you?" I said.

"I received the final draft of the contract you've been working on, and I've gone through it. Everything is in order, and I'm ready to proceed," Dawn replied.

I responded, "That's fantastic news!" I said. "I'm glad you're satisfied. So, what would you like to do next?"

"I hope to come in and sign the papers as soon as possible," Dawn stated.

We finalized our meeting time and exchanged pleasantries. I ended the call and took a moment to gather the necessary documents for Dawn's visit.

Persistent ringing disrupted the gentle office hum once again. I glanced at the screen for an incoming call. I answered, assuming it was Dawn with potential last-minute questions for tomorrow's meeting.

"Hello, Dawn?" I said, prepared to address any additional concerns she might have.

Much to my astonishment, the voice on the other end did not belong to Dawn. "Hey, Holli, Breanna's tone carried an unmistakable urgency, resonating with a palpable energy.

My brows furrowed in confusion as I adjusted to the unexpected change. "Breanna? What's going on?" I asked, my curiosity interested.

"I'm about to interview Cyndi Fontaine, a former worker from EthicalEdge Solutions. She claims to have overheard something significant opening up this case. I need your expertise."

My heart raced at Breanna's words. I stood up from my desk, my mind shifting gears. "I'm on my way. Send me the address."

Breanna texted me the location, and I retrieved my coat, prepared to join her in this pivotal moment. The exasperating week of challenges I had faced at the law firm faded into the background as adrenaline ignited within me. We had been laboring for this opportunity, and I was poised to lend my knowledge to the unfolding dialogue.

Anticipation replaced the frustration that plagued me moments ago. Arriving at the location Breanna sent me, I found myself outside a small, unassuming cafe. Breanna had already arrived, sitting at a corner table, her laptop open in front of her. She looked up and smiled as I approached.

"Thanks for coming, Holli," she greeted me. "Cyndi should be here any minute."

The cafe door opened. An attractive middle-aged woman came into the cafe. Her presence carried a sense of quiet strength, and her warm smile put us at ease. She was wearing a crisp blouse and tailored pants, exuding confidence. Her graying hair pulled back into a ponytail, framing her friendly face.

Recognizing the woman, Breanna waved her over. "You must be Cyndi," Breanna said with a smile.

The woman replied, "Yes. I am Cyndi Fontaine."

Breanna and I exchanged introductions and sensed Cyndi's eagerness to share her story. She recounted her role at EthicalEdge Solutions as we settled into our seats. She explained she worked in the company's supply chain department, coordinating orders and deliveries.

"During one of the company's meetings, I overheard a conversation that chilled me to the bone," Cyndi began, her voice steady but tinged with emotion. "They remained unaware of my presence as I walked in to grab a piece of paper off the copier. I overheard the CEO of Ethical Edge Solutions, Jeff Paulson, and the CEO of Global Sale Wholesaler, William Donavan, discussing using EthicalEdge Solutions as a front to purchase apparel at dirt-cheap prices. An opportunity to make significant profits by leveraging the company's charitable connections and celebrity endorsements. The worst part is they planned to siphon off some of those earnings for themselves."

"Did they say anything else?" I asked.

"Jeff asked William about Dillian Turner's awareness of his responsibilities in handling the 'situation,'" Cyndi continued. "After hearing this, I made sure I left unnoticed."

"Dillion?" Breanna asked.

Cyndi added, "Dillian is Donavan's right-hand man. These are the people who run the sweatshops all over the world."

This revelation was even more damning than we anticipated. Cyndi's firsthand account linked the exploitative practices to the business's top executives.

"They thought the organization's positive image and ethical façade would shield them from suspicion," Cyndi continued, her expression of anger. "It sickens me how they were willing to exploit the company's reputation and deceive the public and the charity organizations involved."

Cyndi spoke, her words painted a disturbing picture of the greed and deceit lurking beneath the surface of EthicalEdge Solutions.

Breanna and I exchanged glances, our minds raced with questions as we processed Cyndi's revelation. Breanna was first to speak, her voice steady but tinged with urgency. She leaned forward, her eyes fixed on Cyndi. "Cyndi, thank you for sharing this with us."

My legal instincts kicked in, "Did you capture any specifics about how this scheme would work? Did they mention anything about the profits or kickbacks?"

Cyndi's brows furrowed as she recalled the conversation. "They talked about how they would source the apparel cheaply, from un-ethical suppliers, and market it as 'ethical' to the public. They believed customers would buy into the idea and the company would earn a significant profit margin. Regarding kickbacks, I remember Jeff men-tioning he funneled some of the profits back to him.

Breanna's eyes narrowed, her resolve intensifying. "Did they men-tion anyone else involved in this scheme? Any names or additional details?"

Cyndi hesitated and deliberated on what she should tell. "I didn't receive any specific names mentioned, but they did talk about enlisting the help of certain suppliers and partners willing to participate in unethical practices. It was an orchestrated plan."

My mind racing, and I wanted to ensure we received all the nec-essary information. "Did they discuss any potential risks or concerns about this plan? Do you have any idea when this conversation took place?"

Cyndi's gaze shifted as she recalled the particulars. "They didn't go into specifics but were aware of potential risks. This conversation happened about six months ago before I left the company."

Breanna nodded, her expression resolute. "Thank you. Your information is invaluable. We'll make sure to investigate this matter ."

Cyndi's eyes held a mix of relief and strength. "I couldn't stay silent about this."

I reached out and placed a reassuring hand on Cyndi's arm. "You've done the right thing," I said.

Cyndi smiled, Breanna added, "We'll need your testimony as we proceed. Will you be willing to cooperate and provide more particulars if needed?"

She nodded. "I want justice served. Others may be willing to talk about the same story. Names are David King, Chloe Brown, and Brittany Fletcher. I might be able to find some emails which may help bring these people to justice."

Breanna and I exchanged another meaningful glance, acknowledging the significance of Cyndi's testimony.

Cyndi's voice wavered, and her eyes were filled with relief and apprehension. She shared substantial information and recounted the details, which took an emotional toll on her.

Cyndi managed a small smile, though fatigue was evident on her face. I'll try to reach out to some of my former colleagues. Please, be careful. These people, they won't hesitate to protect their secrets."

Breanna assured her, "We'll be cautious, Cyndi. Your safety is important to us, and we'll do everything we can to ensure your bravery doesn't go unnoticed."

We parted ways, and Breanna exchanged contact information with Cyndi, ensuring to reach out if further questions arose.

I turned to Breanna, my voice steady but determined. "I'll call Rebeccah and tell her what we've just learned. We'll fill Samantha in on Saturday when we all meet."

Breanna nodded in agreement, her expression reflecting the gravity of the situation. "Ok."

The sound of Breanna's car engine faded into the distance. I took a deep breath and reached for my phone. I dialed Rebeccah's number and put the phone to my ear.

The familiar ringing sound filled the car as I navigated the streets. The setting sun painted the sky with hues of pink and orange. The city came alive with the cacophony of honking taxis, the laughter of children playing in the park, and the aroma of street food wafting nearby.

After a few rings, Rebeccah's voice came through on the other end, warm and familiar. "Hey, Holli. What's going on?"

"Rebeccah, I need to talk to you about something important," I began, my voice severe but steady. "Do you have a moment?"

After a brief pause on the other end, Rebeccah's tone shifted to one of concern. "Of course. Is everything okay?"

Taking a deep breath, I recounted our interview with Cyndi, explaining the significant information she shared. The streetlights began flicking on, casting a soft glow over the surroundings.

Rebeccah responded, "Thank you for telling me. Let's regroup on Saturday and discuss our next move."

Chapter 6

The library's architecture, a blend of classic design and modern functionality, stood as a welcoming beacon. Its exterior of red brick and tall windows exuded timeless wisdom, while the glass entry doors hinted at the knowledge and discovery that lay within. The familiar sight of the library stirred memories of childhood visits and countless hours spent lost in the pages of books.

I parked my car and stepped onto the sidewalk. A gentle breeze carried the scents of mown grass and distant rain, hinting at the changing weather. Cool and refreshing, the air provided a contrast to the warmth of the day. The soft rustle of leaves in nearby trees added a touch of nature's melody to the urban symphony.

My footsteps carried me into the library, and I spotted the familiar figures of my friends gathered in a quiet corner. The sight of Breanna's animated gestures, Samantha's focused expression, and Rebeccah's calm presence eased my nerves. The table was strewn with open notebooks, pens, and printed documents. Breanna glanced in my direction, and I responded with a warm smile. Samantha looked up from her notes and nodded in acknowledgment. Rebeccah's gaze met mine.

The library's silence amplified our presence, creating a sacred space where our shared commitment to uncovering the truth held sway. The faint keyboard tapping from a nearby computer station underscored the purposeful stillness, a reminder that we were not alone.

"The information Cyndi provided is crucial," I stated, my tone reflecting seriousness. "We must be cautious. Let's not conclude anything without more evidence."

Breanna's gaze held mine. "Corroboration and additional witnesses are essential."

My brow furrowed in thought. "Exactly. Prioritize those who might have first-hand knowledge. Regarding the financial records, I believe following the money reveals more about their deceit."

My heart raced as Samantha typed on her keyboard, eyes scanning the screen for any lead. There was an air of anticipation in the room, a sense that we were on the brink of a breakthrough.

Suddenly, Samantha's fingers halted, and her eyes widened with realization. "Holli, I think I've found something," she said, her voice tinged with excitement.

Samantha pointed at a series of transactions, her tone now confident. "following the money from EthicalEdge Solutions led to another company called Global Sale Wholesale. I have a list of names of former employees and whistle-blowers."

"Are any of those the ones Cyndi gave us?" Breanna inquired.

"David King, Chloe Brown, and Brittany Fletcher—are all mentioned," Rebeccah confirmed, peering over Samantha's shoulder.

My pulse quickened as I absorbed the significance of her discovery. This was the tangible link we needed, the concrete evidence that would expose the unethical practices we suspected. My fingers clenched the edge of the desk as I fought to contain my excitement, knowing that we were one step closer to unraveling the truth.

With a surge of determination, I nodded to Samantha. "Let's dig deeper into Global Sale Wholesale and find out where the money leads. We might have the key to blow this open."

Rebeccah's eyes sparkled with intrigue. "That's a solid plan."

"We should also consider the broader impact of exposing Jeff and William for their greed and misrepresentations," I mused. "This is more than just one company. It's about upholding ethical standards of transparency."

Rebeccah's stare met mine, understanding passing between us. "We must build an airtight case."

Determined, we gathered around the library table, each armed with a list of names and corresponding phone numbers. The atmosphere charged with anticipation and apprehension, the weight of our investigation bearing down on us. Breanna decided to make the first call to David King. Her fingers danced across her phone's keypad as she dialed. Her brows furrowed, and her lips tightened as she navigated the conversation. The palpable tension in the room amplified with each passing moment.

Breanna looked up at us, her expression a complex blend of frustration and weariness. "No luck. He declined to speak about it."

Rebeccah's experience mirrored Breanna's with Chloe Brown, yielding similar results. Her eyes, confident, now held a hint of anxious uncertainty. The lines of her forehead deepened as she sighed in exasperation.

Taking a deep breath, I dialed the following number on my list for Brittany Fletcher, my heart pounding. The seconds ticked by, and just as I was beginning to think mine would end in the same disappointing way, a voice answered, "Hello?"

I introduced myself and explained our investigation to Brittany. The conversation unfolded, and a sense of cautious optimism emptied inside me. With each chosen word from her end of the line, that optimism began to wane.

Breanna's jaw tightened, her knuckles turning white as she clenched her phone. Rebeccah's fingers drummed on the table, manifesting her inner turmoil. Brittany's voice wavered, and uncertainty and confusion swirled inside me. I exchanged a glance with Breanna and Rebeccah, and it was clear that we were all grappling with mixed emotions. Frustration, weariness, and a growing sense of anxiety in the air shaped the mood in the room.

My voice remained steady as I pressed Brittany for information, my determination unyielding. Breanna's look fixed on me, her eyebrows furrowing deeper with each contradictory detail. Rebeccah's fingers stilled on the table, her eyes narrowing as if trying to decipher the truth hidden between Brittany's words. I thanked Brittany for her time, a faint sense of disappointment lingering in my tone. I hung up the phone, our conflicting findings settling upon us.

"That didn't yield much," I remarked. Brittany contradicted everything Cyndi mentioned last night. It seemed as if she anticipated our call. Her responses appeared too rehearsed."

Breanna's frustration was palpable. Rebeccah's expression mirrored her unease, her stare shifting between us as if searching for answers that remained out of reach.

We huddled around the library table. Anticipation charged the air. I looked down at my computer, discovered a new email, and opened it. The sender's address was info@GSW.com, and the email was not signed. Could this be from an insider knowledge worker who wants to expose Global Sale Wholesale's questionable dealings? Ripples of excitement sparked through the group.

"This may be what we are missing," Breanna whispered.

The email writer connected the company's financial irregularities to a prominent local politician, John Hawthorne. According to the message, he might have been involved in an influence-peddling scheme, with undisclosed transactions from Global Sale Wholesale funding his House Seat. The claim would send shockwaves through the community and national headlines.

The team weighed their options, each member sharing their thoughts on how to pursue this newfound lead. Reaching out to political insiders, digging into campaign finance records, and perhaps even contacting Hawthorne were all on the table. The tantalizing prospect of exposing corruption at the highest levels of government hung in the air, an intoxicating distraction.

Rebeccah broke the silence with a question on everyone's mind, "Do you think this is legitimate?"

Breanna answered, "I'm not sure, but we can't afford to dismiss it outright. Rebeccah and I should arrange a meeting with the councilman."

Samantha said, "I'll start gathering any information I can find on him." After about 15 minutes, Samantha leaned forward, a mischievous glint in her eyes, as she slid a stack of organized financial records across the table toward me. "Holli, I've managed to gather these records from various sources. Give them to your forensic contact. Don't ask me where or how my dear. I tell you, but I would have to shoot you."

I couldn't help but chuckle at Samantha's characteristic flair for discretion. It was a well-known fact among our group that Samantha had a knack for acquiring information without revealing her methods. Breanna and Rebeccah exchanged knowing glances, their lips quirking in amused agreement. We learned not to question Samantha. Her resourcefulness proved to be a valuable asset.

Taking the stack of papers into my hands, I flipped through them, my curiosity intrigued. The numbers, figures, and line items painted a financial tapestry that held the potential to unveil the truth we sought. "Thank you, Samantha. These provide a crucial piece of the puzzle."

Samantha waved off my gratitude with a casual flick of her wrist. "Just doing my part. What's our next move?"

A thoughtful expression crossed my face. "I will contact Daniel Bass at my law firm and give him the information you just gave me. He specializes in forensic corporate finance and will be able to help us decipher the records. If anything is hidden internally in the numbers, he'll find it."

Rebeccah nodded in agreement, her look focused and determined. "Good plan, Holli. In the meantime, Breanna and I will continue our efforts to reconnect with other former employees. We need to consider others."

Gathering our belongings and preparing to leave the library, Samantha couldn't help but inject a touch of her signature dry humor. "Well, ladies, at least our investigation keeps me away from programming toasters and squirrels."

Laughter rippled through the air, a momentary release of tension. With a final glance at the table, where our notes and plans remained, we left the cool evening wrapping around us.

Samantha winked at us. "Remember, the less you question my methods, the better."

Approaching the door to Daniel's office, my heart beat faster. With a steadying breath, I knocked, and his voice invited me inside. The sunlight cast a prolonged shadow on the floor.

Daniel, a seasoned corporate lawyer with quiet authority, sat behind his desk, his salt-and-pepper hair combed and his sharp gaze framed by wire-rimmed glasses. His office exuded professionalism, adorned with dark wood furnishings and leather chairs, whispered as they shifted under the weight of visitors. "Good morning, Holli," Daniel greeted me with curiosity and readiness.

I settled into the chair opposite his desk, my senses attuned to every detail of the room. The faint ticking of a wall clock punctuated the silence as he leaned back, his fingers steepled beneath his chin.

"So, what brings you here today?" he inquired, his voice a blend of professional curiosity and genuine interest.

I began recounting our investigation to Daniel, including the ethical concerns and mounting evidence against EthicalEdge Solutions and Global Sale Wholesale. Daniel's attentive glance never wavered as I spoke, his expression transitioning from focused to contemplative. I passed him a file containing the documents Samantha provided me.

"Will this overwhelm you," I ask.

He smiled reassuringly. "It won't. I should complete the analysis in about two hours."

Thanking him, I walked down the hallway. On my way, I chatted with Ethan, one of the legal assistants, to discuss the upcoming meeting schedule. We exchanged a few words about the workload for the day, the usual hustle and bustle.

Entering my office, I reviewed contracts and addressed pending client inquiries. Thoughts about the investigation lingered in the back of my mind, a continuous stream of questions and pieces of evidence vying for my attention. Amidst the professional tasks, I couldn't shake off the sensation of something crucial evading our grasp in the case.

A glance at the clock reminded me of the impending meeting with the team regarding the new high school football stadium contract. I gathered the necessary paper files and went to the conference room. I entered the conference room, and they were already engaged in the contract. Everyone engrossed in the particulars of the construction clauses and financial agreements.

"Good morning," I greeted, sitting at the table. "How's the progress?"

Natalie, our detail-oriented legal assistant, presented the latest draft of the agreement. "We've been reviewing the timeline and budget allocation clauses. The contingency plan still has some concerns," said Frank, our compliance officer. "We must ensure they're comprehensive enough to cover unforeseen delays or discrepancies."

Olivia, a paralegal, pointed out a few ambiguous clauses. "We should clarify these sections to avoid potential disputes later on."

I nodded in agreement. "Ambiguity in contracts can lead to legal headaches down the road."

We talked more about the contract and the contingency plan. I expressed my gratitude for everyone's input and adjourned the meeting. I smiled, knowing that Justin's football stadium was going according to plan.

The day had been quite emotional, and I needed time to collect my thoughts before returning to Daniel's office. Breathing, I allowed myself a moment of relaxation and focus.

Going towards Daniel's office, colleagues hurried past, papers rustled, and the distant chatter of conversations filled the air. The vibrant energy of the workplace stirred a noticeable sense of purpose inside me.

My footsteps echoed against the polished floor as I approached Daniel's door. I raised my hand, giving a light knock before stepping inside. The muted glow of the office lights cast a calm ambiance, highlighting the array of files scattered across his desk. Daniel glanced up from his computer screen, a warm smile greeting me. The subtle hum of the air conditioning provided a soothing undertone to our conversation.

"Back so soon, Holli?" Daniel inquired, his tone gentle and inviting.

"Yeah, I just wanted to follow up," I replied.

Daniel gestured for me to sit, and I settled into the chair opposite his desk. After a pause, he spoke with a low cadence of legal wisdom. "It's clear that a lot of money has flowed through their accounts, likely from their questionable practices. One detail caught my attention—a name that shouldn't be listed. You would agree." He leaned forward, his eyes locking onto mine. "Attorney Steve Bachman."

Those words dangled in the air. A palpable thread of intrigue wove into the fabric of our conversation. My heart quickened, a rapid staccato in my chest, and an electric surge of astonishment jolted through me.

It wasn't just any name, he uttered—it was the name of my estranged brother, who remained a distant figure, absent from my life for an extended time. A flood of emotions gushed inwardly, blending curiosity and a tinge of apprehension. The revelation opened the door to a past I long buried, a history now intertwined with our relentless pursuit of truth and justice.

Daniel continued to explain the irregularity; his words became a distant hum, consuming my thoughts. Memories of my brother, our shared childhood, and the unspoken distance that had grown between us flooded my mind.

My hands tightened on the chair's armrests. At that moment, I realized that the pursuit led me down a path I hadn't anticipated. Exiting Daniel's office, my mind urged me to take action and confront the unresolved family issues.

Uncertainty lingered in the air, a veil of questions I was unprepared to answer. What to do now? How would I navigate this unexpected twist in our journey? The prospect of seeing my brother again weighed on my mind, layered with anticipation and anxiety.

Time had done little to erase the pain and hurt that festered in its wake. Our paths diverged, and our interactions became memories tinged with unresolved conflicts. The tendrils of the past reached out, intertwining with the present and complicating matters in ways I had never imagined.

Confronting him, reopening old wounds, and unearthing buried grievances placed an additional burden upon me. Seeing him again stirred a whirlwind of emotions—anger, sadness. A flicker of hope that perhaps, in the face of a common cause, we would rebuild bridges.

The stress was undeniable. It encompassed more than the pressure of piecing together a complex puzzle of corporate deceit and unethical practices. It extended to the emotional toll of navigating the uncharted territory of someone who was a part of my past—a now unexpected participant in our investigation.

Chapter 7

Leaving Daniel's office, conflicting feelings and emotions whirled in my mind, each tugging at my focus. The revelation about my brother had landed like a stone in the calm waters of my consciousness, sending ripples of memories and feelings to the surface. Feeling the need for fresh air, I decided to take a drive. Time to ponder my next move and gather my thoughts had arrived. Stepping out onto the city street, the noise of sights and sounds engulfed me.

Sliding into the driver's seat, I started the engine, the purr of the car a comforting backdrop to the turmoil in my mind. The cityscape a tapestry of towering skyscrapers, pedestrians, and blaring horns stretched before me. Removed and unfocused, my gaze navigated the physical world on autopilot.

Revisiting memories with my brother tinged the nostalgia with the bitterness of past conflicts. Anger at the issues between us battled a desire to bridge the gap that had widened over the years.

Should I extend an olive branch to my brother, attempting to mend the fractures of our past and risking the resurfacing of old wounds?

I needed to prioritize the intensity of the investigation, compartmentalizing my personal history in favor of the overarching mission. These options sprawled ahead of me as divergent paths shrouded in ambiguity and brimming with a web of outcomes.

The news of my brother's involvement in the financial records introduced an added layer of complexity. Opting to confront him about his ties to Global Sale Wholesale may lead to uncomfortable conversations and challenging revelations, and avoiding this dialogue might cultivate a sense of guilt.

Returning to my office, I pulled into the parking lot of my building, and a decision had taken root in me. A sense of clarity had emerged from the storm. Sitting alone in my office, the weight of my decision bore down on me, an unrelenting force as heavy as a ton of bricks. Its implications could unravel my life and the fabric of our ongoing investigation.

Should I reach out to Steve? There was no assurance of his willingness to cooperate or his readiness to unveil the truth about his participation with Global Sale Wholesale. Our shared history is tainted by bitterness and unresolved conflicts. I couldn't dismiss the grim possibility that he might prioritize self-preservation and the clandestine dealings of the company over any remnants of family loyalty.

With determination, I reached for my phone and dialed Rebeccah's number. It rang each tone, a reminder of the impending conversation. Her voice, a welcome anchor amid the storm of my thoughts, provided solace when she answered.

"Hey, Rebeccah. I need to talk to you, Breanna, and Samantha. Can we set up a meeting?"

Rebeccah's tone held a note of concern. "Of course, Holli. Is everything alright?"

Taking a deep breath, steadying myself for what lay ahead. "There's something I need to share. Let's meet at my office tonight. I'll explain everything then."

We arranged the details, and as I ended the call, I felt a sense of resolution. The uncertainty still lingered, but I had made a choice—to face my past and to find a way to move forward.

The door to my office swung open, and the soft rustle of clothing and hushed whispers announced the arrival of my friends. Breanna, Samantha, and Rebeccah entered, their presence a comforting reassurance amidst the weight of the day's decisions. Their expressions held a mix of curiosity, concern, and unwavering support.

The evening light filtered through the window blinds, casting elongated patterns across the floor. Breanna's determined gaze met mine. Her shoulders squared with resolve. Samantha's eyes held a glimmer of anticipation, while Rebeccah's calm demeanor exuded a sense of steady assurance.

Rebeccah shared the meeting with Councilman Hawthorne, and she commented, "It didn't take long for the conversation to go nowhere. He stuck to the classic politician's script, repeating 'no comment' and 'I have no recollection.'"

"A textbook politician 'cause he is down in the polls," I added.

Samantha chimed in, determination in her voice. "It's time to dive into the digital trail. If there's anything to uncover about our Councilman Hawthorn and misdeeds, I'll track it down."

We gathered around my desk, the polished surface held a scattering of notes, files, and a laptop—a visual representation of the complexity of our investigation. The air, thick with anticipation, enveloped us as we sat. We were strategically positioned to face the center, where I would soon share what had been gnawing in my mind.

Daniel's uncovered information detailed thousands of dollars flowing through overseas banks. The enormity of what we discovered settled upon me, and the mention of an anonymous attorney's involvement added an electrifying jolt to the room. This was a turning point, a potential key to unlocking the truth behind the tangled web of EthicalEdge Solutions' unethical dealings.

The weight of that fact pressed upon me, a sense of responsibility and urgency intertwining in my mind. Additionally, I informed the women that I had taken the initiative to engage Amanda, our research assistant. I reached out to her, hope and uncertainty churning. Uncovering crucial details about the anonymous attorney's background and motivations induced a sense of nervous tension. She unearthed a trove of telling details. I had to process this new data to come up with some conclusions.

Breanna's impatience was like a drumbeat in the room, her urgency infused the space with an electric charge as she advocated for immediate action, and her words were laced with passion and conviction.

"Time to wait is over," Breanna declared, her voice tinged with frustration. "We need to expose every ounce of this right now. Let's write a story that shines a blazing spotlight on these unethical practices and doesn't hesitate to name this attorney."

Rebeccah's empathetic presence radiated beside her. I took a deep breath, mustering the strength to voice the most astonishing twist.

"We can't reveal his name," I declared. "The attorney's name is Steve Bachman—my brother."

A collective gasp echoed through the room, and widened eyes met mine. The impact of my statement was immediate, and a wave of astonishment and understanding swept over us. Breanna's impatience softened, replaced by a mixture of surprise and realization.

I shared Daniel and Amanda's findings with the group, the words hanging like a bridge between the present and the past. Soft lamplight painted warm, shifting patterns on the walls, creating a cozy ambiance in the room. The sun sank below the horizon, fading rays casting long, elongated shadows. The subtle hum of the air conditioning and the sounds of city life supported our hushed conversation.

"Steve was William's attorney during his time at Global Sale Wholesale," I explained, my voice a mixture of intrigue and trepidation. "His name shows in both legitimate deposits and some suspicious."

Rebeccah's practicality shone through; her solution-oriented mind quickly offered suggestions. "Let's just give him a call, Holli. He might have the answers we need."

"It's not that simple, Rebeccah," I admitted, my gaze drifting toward the window. "Indeed, Steve and I haven't spoken in years, there's more to it than that. Our relationship soured over a bitter dispute about our parents' estate and inheritance, but other layers to our history complicate matters."

The words hung in the air, an unspoken weight that settled on each of us. Breanna's expression was a blend of understanding and concern, her features softened by the revelation. Samantha's mind was connecting the dots between family discord and potential financial misconduct. Rebeccah's empathetic gaze met mine, acknowledging the situation's complexity.

I spoke up, my voice steady, "I'll be taking a trip to Cedarwood Springs to visit my brother."

Rebeccah asked, "Do you want us to come with you?" Breanna and Samantha echoed her sentiment with supportive nods.

Managing a small smile, touched by their unspoken well wishes. I replied, "Thank you, but I must face this alone."

We concluded our meeting with a mix of anticipation and uncertainty hanging in the air. Breanna, Samantha, and Rebeccah expressed their understanding and support for my decision to confront my past and seek answers from my brother.

Chapter 8

Cruising down the highway, the passing scenery painted a tableau of rural beauty. Rolling hills stretched far, with their lush greenery and gentle slopes. The occasional farmhouse dotted the landscape, its weathered charm a testament to the passage of time. Tranquility settled over me, and the solitude offered a space for contemplation.

The music played through the car's speakers, creating a harmonious blend of engines and the whoosh of the wind. The road stretched before me, leading me closer to Cedarwood Springs. My thoughts embarked on a journey of their own, wandering back to when my brother Steve and I were inseparable. The current situation lifted for a moment as the warmth of those cherished memories enveloped me.

One vivid recollection transported me to the day of my law school graduation. The air crackled with an electric sense of achievement. Amid the sea of proud families and graduates, Steve's beaming smile stood out, mirroring my joy. His presence was a rock of unwavering support during the celebration.

Following the ceremony, our embrace was laughter and triumph, harmonizing with the jubilant cheers around us. "Holli, you did it!" Steve's voice, infused with genuine pride, exclaimed, "You're a lawyer now."

My grin mirrored his, a blend of relief and accomplishment flooding me. "I owe a lot of this to you. Your constant encouragement and unwavering belief carried me through."

The connection between us was palpable as we revisited the path that led me to that moment. We recounted tales of struggles, hopes, and aspirations, basking in the glow of our success.

Another memory surfaced, tied to the day I passed the bar exam. I dialed Steve's number almost before the results sunk in, my voice trembling with excitement and nervousness. "Guess what, Steve? I did it! I passed the bar!"

His exuberant cheer resonated through the phone, echoing his unshakable confidence in me. "Holli, that's incredible! Here comes a force to deal with," he declared.

His unwavering belief was a wellspring of strength, a reminder I maintained a steadfast ally no matter the challenge. My thoughts then shifted to the day I moved into my first apartment in Sunnyville. Excitement charged the air as Steve and I hauled boxes and furniture up the stairs. Laughter filled the air within those four walls, transforming the unpacking into an adventure. His playful teasing made the transition into independent living bearable.

"Welcome to the world of grown-up responsibilities, sis," Steve grinned, his eyes reflecting pride and sibling camaraderie. "Just promise you won't forget your older, wiser brother now you're a hotshot lawyer."

We reminisced late into the night, trading stories of our childhood antics and painting vivid future pictures. Those moments became the bedrock of our bond, nurturing a deep reservoir of experiences and unspoken understanding.

Continuing toward Cedarwood Springs, the shifting landscape outside mirrored the transformation of time itself. The scenery outside my car window blurred as my thoughts carried me to a pivotal moment. The air held the crispness of fall, and the trees adorned themselves in a rich tapestry of amber and gold. It was a season of change, nature's gradual transition into a quieter state. The once-fond memories of my brother began to merge with a more tumultuous period in my family's history—a time marked by stress and upheaval. My mind guided me back five years to a taxing and challenging chapter—my mother's passing and the aftermath of settling her estate alongside my brother, Steve.

The hospital corridors were a maze of hushed conversations and antiseptic scents, contrasting the vibrant energy my mother exuded. Tubes and monitors became a dissonant symphony, a constant reminder of the fragility of life. My mother has been my role model, a pillar of strength and grace. She navigated life's challenges with a tenacity that left me in awe. Her health began deteriorating, and I paused my career, choosing to be by her in her final year.

She slipped away in the gentlest of whispers, surrounded by the loving embrace of her family. Beside her, my brother stood firm, a united front of aunts, cousins, and dear family friends, creating a circle of support. Her breaths grew faint in those sacred moments as the essence of transition unfolded before us. The profound stillness held a sense of serenity, a quiet passage I believed led her to the waiting arms of God, where she would find solace and peace.

Recalling the day I left our childhood home to sort out the details of my inheritance—a task fallen to me as my mother's closest confidante.

My brother, Steve, stood in the doorway, his expression a blend of uncertainty and apprehension.

"You're going through with this, Holli?" he asked, his voice tinged with disbelief and concern.

I met his gaze, determination in my eyes. "Mom's wishes are clear, Steve. She entrusted me with this responsibility, which I intend to honor."

He sighed, his shoulders slumping. "It's just... I thought these decisions were made together, as a family."

The tension of conflict pulled at my heart. "Steve, Mom made it clear she wanted me to take the lead. She believed in me, and I can't let her down."

The conversation lingered in the air, an unspoken understanding of the emotional stakes. A nod of reluctant acceptance met my decision, and I left with determination and a tinge of guilt.

The memories of time served as a poignant backdrop. The drive was more than just a physical journey. It was a pilgrimage into the past, a quest to confront the tangled web of the investigation and the unresolved threads of my history. The road stretched out ahead. A path of introspection and discovery would lead me to face my brother and unearth the truth beneath the surface.

Approaching Steve's home in Cedarwood Springs, a sense of uncertainty clung to the edges of my thoughts, mingling with the anticipation that accompanied me on the drive. Nestled among towering trees, the house exuded an air of comfort and familiarity. The late afternoon sun cast a warm, golden hue across the front yard, where the grass swayed in greeting. The soft rustling of leaves and the distant chirping of birds created a soothing backdrop. A natural symphony enveloped the scene.

The gravel path crunched beneath my tires as I pulled into the driveway, and I took a moment to steady my breathing before stepping out of the car. The air carried earthy notes of soil and vegetation, hints of blooming flowers, and the subtle aroma of wood from the nearby trees. It was a fragrance speaking of nature's embrace, of the simple yet profound beauty of the world around us.

With a deep breath, I approached the front door, my heart beating a little faster as I raised my hand to knock. The rhythmic sound echoed through the air, and each tap was a harbinger of the unknown. The door swung open moments later, revealing Steve on the other side. His eyes mixed with surprise and curiosity, and a small smile tugged at the corners of his lips.

"Holli?" he said, his voice laced with disbelief and warmth.

A flood of emotions surging. "Yes, Steve, it's me," I replied, my voice blending nervousness and affection.

We stood for a moment, taking in each other's presence. Steve's arms opened and I stepped into a hug like a reunion of hearts. The embrace was warm and familiar, a testament to the bond despite the passage of time.

"It's been too long," Steve murmured, affirming our sentiment.

Nodding, blinking back the sudden welling of tears. "Yes," I agreed, my throat tight with emotion.

We pulled back from the hug, I met Steve's gaze, and a softness in his eyes spoke volumes. The years of distance and unresolved tensions faded into the background, replaced by an understanding of the complexity of our relationship.

"Come in, Holli," Steve said, stepping aside to usher me into the warmth of his home.

A sense of nostalgia washed over me. Familiar touches adorn the house's interior. On this cozy couch, countless conversations, a bookshelf filled with volumes we enjoyed, and photographs capturing our past.

The sound of a kettle whistling in the kitchen added to the ambiance, and the aroma of brewed tea wafted through the air. It was a simple gesture, yet it held a world of unspoken comfort—a gesture spoke of the bond before life has taken us on separate paths. We settled in the living room with tea cups in hand, the awkwardness gave way to a more relaxed atmosphere.

"Steve," I managed, my voice betraying emotions. "I must say, your style evolved."

He chuckled, a warmth in his eyes mirrored his smile. "Well, life changes us."

Tasteful decorations adorned the interior, blending modern elements with inviting, cozy touches. The faint aroma of a home-cooked meal hung in the air, a reminder of the domesticity I hadn't associated with Steve before.

The atmosphere of his home was at odds with the memories I had held onto for years. The tension I braced for was absent, replaced by an unexpected ease.

"Steve," I began, my gaze meeting his. "I must admit, I wasn't quite expecting this."

He nodded. "I understand, Holli. We have our history, and putting it aside isn't easy. Time shifts perspectives."

His words struck a chord, resonating with my reflection and introspection. The past disagreements and the longing for resolution were palpable in the space between us.

"Time and reflection," he continued, his voice carrying a note of contemplation. "They've given me a new outlook on things. Life's too short to hold onto grudges with family."

I nodded, the turmoil giving way to a flicker of hope. "A fresh start," I murmured, the words carrying their weight.

Steve's eyes held a sincerity reaching beyond words. "Holli, I've missed having you in my life. I've missed the bond we used to have. I want to try to rebuild it."

Tears pricked at the corners of my eyes, welling up. The desire for reconciliation, the possibility of bridging the gap that kept us apart, was overwhelming and exhilarating.

"I've missed it too," I admitted, my voice catching. "Our bond, the laughter, the support. I've missed having my brother by my side."

With vulnerability and determination, I took a deep breath. "Steve, I want to start by apologizing for my role in our time apart. Our disagreements were two-way, and I take responsibility for letting our differences drive a wedge between us."

His gaze softened, a mixture of understanding and appreciation in his eyes. "Holli, I appreciate it. I apologize, too. Letting things fester and not reaching out to you sooner—it's a regret I've carried for years."

We settled into a natural conversation. We discussed our challenges, the moments we missed sharing, and the longing to rebuild our relationship.

"I've been thinking," I said, "We can establish a routine to keep in better touch. Regular calls, or even just messages, to check in and share what's happening in our lives."

Steve nodded, a thoughtful expression on his face. "I like the idea. Plan some visits, too. It's been too long since we've spent quality time together."

A sense of hope blossomed within me as we discussed the practical steps to nurture our rekindled bond. The prospect of having my brother back in my life, not just as a family member but as a friend and confidant, was like a gift I hadn't dared to hope for.

Our conversation flowed, and Steve's curiosity led him to inquire about my professional life. "So, where are you practicing law these days, Holli? In what department?"

Smiling, appreciating his interest. "I'm working at Winston & Associates, a law firm in Sunnyville. I'm part of the corporate law department, focusing on contract negotiations and compliance."

His eyebrows raised in genuine intrigue. "Impressive. It sounds like you're doing some important work."

I nodded, proud to share this aspect of my life with him. "It's challenging but rewarding. What about you? How's life been treating you?"

"Holli, after some soul-searching and reflection, I decided to shift in my career. I've moved away from contracts and finances, and now I'm focusing on a different area of law."

Curiosity grabbed me, and I leaned forward. "Oh? What area are you working in now?"

He replied with pride, "I'm a bankruptcy attorney now. It's been a significant change, but I'm directly impacting people's lives, helping them navigate difficult financial situations."

Admiring his decision to transition into an area of law focused on compassion and assistance, I said, "That's admirable, Steve. It takes courage to overcome those challenges and support others during such times."

He nodded, showing a sense of contentment in his expression. "I've found a deeper sense of purpose in this work. It's about giving people a chance for a fresh start, which I believe in."

Our conversation continued. Steve spoke about his past involvement with a wholesale clothing store. "You remember how I used to work for the clothing store, right?" He sighed, a hint of regret in his tone. "Things took a turn, Holli. I couldn't ignore issues within the company —ethical issues and financial mismanagement. I made a decision and stepped away."

I took advantage of this unbelievable moment to address the topic I came for—"Steve," I began, my voice measured, "To be honest, this is one of the reasons I came over today. The company you used to work for, Global Sale Wholesale, I just found out is involved in some questionable practices. Reports of corruption, kickbacks, and unethical dealings." I continued, "What's even more concerning is the indications some of those kickbacks are going to EthicalEdge Solutions."

Steve asked, "How did you stumble on this information?"

I recounted the investigation to Steve, letting him know the details and how it all began.

His eyes widened in surprise, his expression shock and disbelief. "Wait, you're saying they were planning to give kickbacks to EthicalEdge?"

Nodding. "Yes, that's what the evidence suggests." I hesitated before continuing, my heart pounding with the next revelation. "Steve, your name came up concerning these financial transactions. Your name appears on many documents related to these transactions."

His eyes searched mine, flickering across his features—surprise, concern, and perhaps a touch of guilt. "My name? I had no idea about any of this, Holli."

"I trust you, Steve. This doesn't sound like you at all," I reassured him. "There are various ways your name got tangled up in those records. The one coming to my mind is fraud."

Steve nodded. "I wouldn't put it past them. They're a shady group." Steve's brow furrowed, and his jaw tensed as he absorbed the allegations. "Wow. Kickbacks to Ethical Edge," he said. I nodded, allowing the gravity of the situation to sink in.

With a steadying breath, my tone softened yet resolute: "Steve, I understand this is overwhelming, but I must ask you—were you ever receiving any funds from these transactions? I'm also curious about your specific role in the company. Can you provide any evidence helping establish your non-involvement and refute any connection to these financial activities?"

With a composed demeanor, Steve met my gaze and began to share his side of the story. "Holli, I never received any funds from those transactions or kickbacks. My role at Global Sale Wholesale focused on contract negotiation and legal matters. I ensured the company's business dealings were sound and compliant."

His voice carried sincerity and frustration. "My departure from the wholesale clothing business, certain ethical concerns and practices emerged. I realized staying there compromised my values and couldn't be a part of it. Confidentiality agreements prevented me from disclosing specific details."

"I may face disciplinary action, or worse, be disbarred," Steven commented.

"Are any names of individuals linked to these financial documents?" I inquired, locking my gaze with his.

"I'm not sure, but consider looking into Tiffany Burlson. She held the position of lead accountant during my tenure," he replied.

Sensing a mixture of relief and sincerity in his words. The truth hung in the air, a delicate balance between seeking answers and preserving the fragile bond we were attempting to rebuild.

I realized the complexity of the situation. My brother, the man I grew up with, who had been by my side through many pivotal moments, was entangled in allegations and deceit. I watched his earnest expression and the vulnerability in his gaze, I couldn't help but experience a surge of empathy. My heart tore between the duty to uncover the truth and the desire to believe in the innocence of the person before me. The emotions swirling were a tumultuous mix—confusion, concern, and an overwhelming need to understand the reality of the situation.

Steve and I stood on his porch, our conversation hanging between us. His eyes held a blend of gratitude, relief, and a hint of apprehension, mirroring the whirlwind I was experiencing.

"I appreciate you coming all this way, Holli," Steve said, his voice sincere. This conversation means a lot to me."

My heart heavy with the past and future possibilities. "I'm glad we talked, Steve. Remember, I will do everything I can to uncover the truth. I'll find it, give you the evidence, and clear your name."

He nodded, a mixture of gratitude and determination in his expression. "Thank you, Holli. We don't have to wait for the investigation to visit each other again. How about we plan to meet in Sunnyville? We should catch up."

The suggestion warmed my heart, shining through the shadows of uncertainty. "Wonderful, Steve. Let's do it. I'll call you when I'm back in town, and we can make arrangements."

The drive home was a blur of memories, the setting sun casting long shadows as I wrestled with nostalgia, determination, and a thirst for answers. Reaching for my phone, I dialed Samantha's number, my fingers tapping on the steering wheel. The phone rang, and growing anticipation. Samantha's voice came through the line, like a lifeline connecting me to the next chapter of our investigation.

"Hey, Samantha," I greeted. "I need a favor. Please check on someone for me. Her name is Tiffany Burlson, and she's the former accountant of Global Sale Wholesale. I have a hunch she might hold some valuable information."

Through the phone, Samantha's mischievous giggle rang in my ear, "I am also researching our buddy John Hawthorne. I found out he is dirty, but nothing substantial yet!"

Chuckling, I replied, "Good job, Samantha. I will remember not to ask you where or how you get your information. Don't worry, your secret's safe with me. You've got some spy skills."

Samantha's laughter bubbled through the line, "Well, a girl's got to have her secrets."

"Oh," I agreed with a grin. "You, my friend, are the queen of enigma."

Samantha groaned, "I should put it on my business card."

"You should!" I commented. "I will talk with you when I am in town."

Chapter 9

Dialing Daniel's number with determined fingers. The ringing echoed in my ears, reverberating. The world seemed to suspend its breath, acutely aware of the call's gravity.

"Hello?" Daniel's voice carried through the receiver, a bridge between two worlds.

"Daniel," I began, my voice steady yet laced with the moment's thrill. "It's Holli. How have you been?"

The familiarity in his manner brought a smile to my lips. "Holli! I'm doing well, thank you. How about you?"

A rush of emotions surged within me, a blend of eagerness and nerves, as I responded, "I'm doing well too. Listen, Daniel, I once again find myself in need of your expertise. Those financial documents I provided you with – the ones related to Global Sale Wholesale – I need your help with some more forensic accounting."

A moment of silence hung before Daniel's thoughtful voice replied, "Are we looking into potential irregularities?"

"Yes," I confirmed, my fingers tracing an absent pattern on the table's surface. "I spent Saturday talking with Steve about the documents. He insists he is not involved and claims it was all orchestrated by William Donavan and Jeff Paulson."

The gears of Daniel's mind turned, his response broken by contemplation. "William Donavan and Jeff Paulson? That adds an intriguing layer to the puzzle. This afternoon, I'll delve into the documents."

"I'm also working with someone gathering more data," I added. "Can I forward it to you?"

Daniel affirmed, his demeanor a reassuring anchor. "I'll incorporate it into my analysis. Expect results as soon as I can manage."

"Thank you, Daniel," I said, gratitude and determination mingling in those words.

Sitting back in my chair, relief and anticipation washed over me. I settled into my office, my phone buzzed with an incoming call. Glancing at the screen, I spotted Justin's name. We hadn't spoken since our encounter at the fundraiser, and I sensed a flicker of curiosity as I answered. After exchanging pleasantries, Justin's voice carried a sense of purpose.

"Holli, I've meant to catch up with you," he began. "How about we discuss a few things, including those contracts?"

A smile curved my lips. "That sounds like a great idea, Justin. Let's do it. What time and what day works for you?"

"How about right now?" he proposed.

"Let me ask Mark. I understand you'll want to meet him." I replied.

"Sure, I'll go ahead and hold so you can ask," he responded.

Dialing Mark's extension, I asked, "Mark, Justin wants to meet. Do you have time?

"Of course," he responded. "He happens to be my favorite client."

Picking up the line Justin was on, "That will be fine, Justin. See you when you arrive."

With its organized chaos of papers and files, my desk stood ready to receive my attention. I found myself immersed in contract details. The collaborative venture between the high school and the Youth Sports and Education Alliance for the new stadium project had been in the works for months. It was a massive undertaking, and my role as legal counsel was crucial in ensuring the project's success. I delved into the intricate details of the contracts, and my office phone rang.

"Morning, Holli," Joseph Flanigan greeted me. He was our go-to liaison with the high school, and his enthusiasm for the stadium project was contagious.

"Good morning, Joseph," I replied with a smile. "I had a meeting with my team, and it appears that everything is going according to plan. How are things on your end?"

Joseph's voice crackled with eagerness. "That sounds fantastic! The groundbreaking ceremony is just around the corner, and the community is buzzing. We couldn't have reached this point without you, Holli."

My focus remained on the task. "I'm glad to learn that, Joseph. Let's make sure everything is buttoned up before the ceremony."

Justin's entrance into my office brought a distinct unease. He appeared troubled, and I started to recount the conversation I'd just had with Joseph. Before I could dive into it, Justin seemed preoccupied with another matter.

He began. "I've been hearing unsettling rumors about a company I'm involved with for my clothing line, Global Sale Wholesale."

"What's prompting this concern now?" I inquired, intrigued by his sudden focus.

He explained, "My agent just warned me that if there's any misconduct or any wrongdoing, it could affect my image. That's why I brought in my EthicalEdge Solutions for the ad campaign—to reassure everyone that my products are ethical and don't rely on sweatshops or child labor."

I answered, "I didn't realize you had any connection with them. They're under investigation, and it's not looking positive. Your best bet would be to consult your attorneys. Is this what you wanted to discuss with me? I can handle the necessary paperwork if you decide to cut ties with them."

He nodded in acknowledgment. "Yea, I think I should talk to my attorneys."

"I believe that's a great idea," I affirmed.

Thanking Justin for coming by, I walked him to Mark's office and excused myself as I returned to mine. I experienced relief, knowing the wheels were set in motion to address the potential challenges ahead. The papers on my desk held a new layer of significance now, each document representing not just legal jargon but a piece of the broader puzzle unfolding before me.

My thoughts wandered, and a sudden ring suddenly broke the silence, the phone demanding attention. It was a call from Samantha, Rebeccah, and Breanna, their voices merging through the speakerphone on Rebeccah's end.

"Quick, Holli, it's lunchtime! Come over to Samantha's apartment," she exclaimed with palpable enthusiasm. "We believe we've found the evidence to bring Paulson and Donavan down and put them behind bars for a long time."

Hearing this, I abandoned my office and went. I approached the front door. I stepped inside her apartment, where the air buzzed with excitement. Rebeccah, Samantha, and Breanna greeted me with broad smiles and animated gestures, their eyes gleaming.

"What's the thrilling news?" I asked, a smile mirroring their own. "I'm a bit left out here. Fill me in!"

Samantha took the lead, her voice carrying a hint of mischief. "I've managed to uncover some pretty damning evidence about William. I've got an internal email from Tiffany Burlson discussing their plan to make, and I quote, a boatload of money off the backs of these ungrateful children."

"My brother came through for us," I said.

Rebeccah followed up, saying, "He made a significant contribution!"

Breanna jumped in, her tone more somber. "Another email reveals they had no intention of fixing up the factories. "They aimed to implement a 14-hour workday for mere pennies on the dollar. It's horrifying."

I inquired, "What about Councilman Hawthorne?"

Samantha responded, "He's as corrupt as they come in politics, but he's not involved. Whoever provided the details wanted us to divert our attention to him instead of our original lead. We are still unsure of the email's sender, but Councilman Hawthorne will likely be stepping down soon, and Representative Hawthorne is not in the future," she added with a wink.

Absorbing their revelations. "I'm thrilled," I acknowledged. "Where does this leave my brother? Was he involved in any of this?"

"Pass this to Daniel," Samantha advised, her voice serious. I discovered more detailed financial records here. Maybe he can connect the dots." With a wink, she added, "You've no idea where it came from."

Laughter erupted, filling the room with an infectious energy.

"Guess what, everyone?" I stated suddenly. "Justin visited me this morning. The receiver from the Emerald City Thunderhawks? He's been using Global Sale Wholesale for his clothing line and EthicalEdge to market them. He might be severing ties with them."

A chorus of gasps and intrigued glances swept through the group, creating a ripple of surprise that echoed around the room. Eyes widened in shared astonishment as each of us absorbed the unexpected revelation. Rebeccah's eyebrows arched upwards, clearly showing her heightened interest and focused attention. Her curiosity sparked as she sought to delve deeper into the newfound knowledge. Breanna and Samantha's faces became a canvas of emotions, where astonishment and realization mingled to form a complex yet compelling expression.

"That's not all," I continued, the suspense in the air almost palpable. "He wants to ensure that everything is legit and that he isn't tied to wrongdoing."

Rebeccah's voice broke the brief silence, her question hanging in the air. "So, what's our next move? Where do we go from here?"

Leaning forward, my gaze focused and determined. "First, we wait for Daniel's analysis of the financial files. Forensic accounting will be our compass, pointing us toward where we should follow the money trail."

Breanna's eyes gleamed. "I might take this to the media. It's been a while since I've worked on an investigative story, and I feel the network would be all over this."

Rebeccah's expression turned thoughtful, her resolve unwavering. "I need to begin to prepare a presentation to the Board of Directors. It's becoming clear that a resignation might not be too far off. It's a shame. I enjoyed working for him."

Samantha grinned and shrugged. "Well, you know what they say, a little drama and suspense make everything more exciting – even exposing corporate misdeeds!"

Concluding our lunch, the room reverberated with the harmonious symphony of laughter and camaraderie, a testament to the deepening connection that had flourished between us. Retrieving my keys, I bid my farewells, enveloping each of my companions with promising smiles.

Emotions stirred within me – a mix of enthusiasm, hope, and determination. I navigated the bustling city streets, my mind replayed the scene at Samantha's apartment. The earnest expressions on their faces and the palpable excitement that permeated the room were a testament to the power of collaboration.

I dropped off Samantha's data for forensic accounting. The anticipation hung in the air, both of us aware of the data's significance and potential. With the documents in hand, I outlined the request, my voice steady but charged with the situation's urgency.

"Daniel," I began, "Here is the additional information I told you about. I need your expertise in connecting the dots and compiling this into a comprehensive report."

His attentive gaze met mine as he accepted the documents, a shared understanding passing between us. He posed a question on his mind, his curiosity genuine and probing. "Holli, where did you manage to obtain this?"

I responded with a playful glint danced in my eyes, my words laced with a hint of mystery. "Oh, you know how it goes, Daniel. I've got my sources, and they're solid. Let's say I've got a friend. Can't reveal too much, but it's legitimate."

A chuckle escaped Daniel's lips, his laughter a familiar sound that resonated with camaraderie. "Ah, the mysterious informant. We all have at least one of those friends, don't we? Well, I'll trust your judgment on this, Holli."

With a nod of mutual understanding, I bid Daniel farewell and stepped out of his office. Taking a deep breath, I picked up the phone and dialed Steve's number. My fingers trembled as each ring echoed in my ear. He answered, a mix of relief and urgency filled my voice. "Steve, I've got news," I said, my words quivering. "We've uncovered something big in the investigation. We've uncovered substantial evidence like emails and testimonies. It's strong enough to implicate both Jeff and William."

Silence hung on the line for a moment, a pregnant pause laden with the weight of understanding. Steve's voice, a blend of hope and caution, broke through. "Holli, that's incredible news. I must find out if my name is clear, and I'm no longer under suspicion."

My heart ached at his concern, his desire for vindication palpable even through the phone. "Steve, we're working on it. The evidence we've gathered so far doesn't implicate you. We're focusing on ensuring that it is cleared definitively. You've always maintained your innocence, and we're determined to prove it."

His exhale held a mix of relief and trepidation. "I trust you, Holli. Thank you for everything you're doing."

"We won't stop until we clear your name."

After the call concluded, I reclined in my chair, a whirlwind of emotions dancing within me. The weight of responsibility and the unbreakable bond of sibling love propelled me forward with a renewed sense of purpose. Retrieving my purse and keys, I set out for the parking lot. The weariness from the day's strain and emotional tumult lingered, leaving me yearning for solace. I set aside thoughts of Justin's contracts, the ongoing investigation, and the imperative task of restoring my brother's tarnished reputation.

I needed to be home, a sanctuary for my soul, where I shed the armor I wear in the outside world, embrace vulnerability, reflect, rejuvenate, and find the strength to face challenges. It's a place of authenticity, where my true self is.

Chapter 10

The early morning light bathed the room in a gentle glow, tracing delicate patterns on the furniture and infusing the space with a muted warmth. It was a quiet haven imbued with the calm of dawn. Outside, the soft chirping of birds intertwined, composing a tranquil symphony that painted the backdrop to this serene moment.

A sharp knock pierced the stillness, shattering the peaceful ambiance. My heart skipped a beat, the sound jolting me from my slumber's embrace. I sat up, eyes fixed on the door as though it held the answers to this unexpected intrusion. The knocking persisted, each rap on the wood resonating.

Casting aside the covers, my bare feet met the cool floor as I swung my legs out of the bed. A yawn escaped my lips as I stretched, my body grappling with the remnants of sleep. Donning my robe, I shuffled toward the source of the disturbance, a mixture of curiosity and caution guiding my steps.

Peering through the peephole, I focused on the blurred figure on the other side. Recognition dawned on me, and a wave of bewilderment surged forth. In the corridor stood my brother. His unexpected presence tugged at my heartstrings, igniting a blend of emotions within me – surprise, concern, and a flicker of joy.

With a slight fumble, the door unlocked, its metallic click resonating. The door swung open, it revealed my brother's tired yet resolute expression.

"Steve?" My voice a mixture of disbelief and warmth, my eyes narrowing as if trying to anchor his figure in reality. "What brings you here?"

Stepping back, a wordless invitation for him to enter, a gesture that carried volumes of unspoken connection. He crossed the threshold into my house, our eyes locked in another silent exchange, a communication of understanding that needed no words.

"Holli," he began. "I had to talk to you in person. Can you clear my name? My entire career is on the line, and the thought of being disbarred terrifies me."

A reassuring smile carved on my lips as our eyes held steady, my determination unwavering. "You know I'll do everything I can to protect your reputation," I assured him. "We've brought in one of the best legal minds to handle forensic accounting. It's a comprehensive strategy. I have absolute faith that you will be vindicated. The exciting part – I have a secret weapon, a friend with an uncanny knack for uncovering insider information."

His eyes lit up with curiosity, and his half-smile indicated his intrigue. "I'd love to meet her."

My grin widened, a playful glint in my eyes. "Well, today's your lucky day. You'll see her and my entire team of friends 'cause we're getting together for lunch."

His eyes danced with a mix of emotions. "An investigation team? You know how to keep things interesting."

"You have no idea," I replied, the playfulness in my tone mirroring the twinkle in my eyes. "Let's sit down for breakfast and catch up. There's so much to discuss."

My heart raced as the phone rang, excitement and curiosity coursing me. "Hello?" I greeted her with professionalism and warmth, recognizing the voice of Justin's administrative assistant, Rayna Zellar, on the other end. "Good morning, Holli. Justin would like to see you today. Are you available?"

Intrigue sparked in my eyes as I processed Rayna's words, my mind racing to decipher the purpose behind Justin's request. "Of course," I responded, my voice steady and attentive. "I'm available. Is there a specific time in mind?" Rayna's voice remained composed, carrying a hint of formality that was characteristic of her role.

"He would like to see you around 2:00 PM at your office if that works for you."

"I'll be expecting him at 2:00 PM. Thank you for letting me know. I'll make sure to inform Mike. He should have those contracts completed and ready to present ."

Sensing my need for clarity, Rayna's tone became more earnest. "Holli, I should clarify. This meeting pertains to another legal matter. It concerns Global Sale Wholesale."

My eyebrows knitted together in thought as I absorbed this new information, my mind working to process its implications. "Understood," I acknowledged. "I'll be prepared and waiting at 2:00 PM. Please let him know that others will also attend the meeting."

With the details settled, Rayna bid me farewell, and I placed the receiver back in its cradle. Tenacity surged through me as I absorbed the weight of the conversation.

A thoughtful silence settled between Steve and me. Our eyes met, and the weight of the impending conversation hung heavy. Curiosity and concern mingled, his brow furrowed as he broke the silence.

"Who's Justin?" he asked, his interest coloring his tone. What's his connection to this Global Sale Wholesale?"

I took a moment to collect my thoughts and met my brother's gaze as I explained. "He is a professional athlete, a wide receiver for the Emerald City Thunderhawks. I am working on the contracts for his charity, and he told me he's been using Global Sale Wholesale to manufacture and EthicalEdge Solutions to market his apparel line.'

Understanding dawned on Steve, a mixture of surprise and realization crossing his expression. "So, Justin's more than just an acquaintance. His involvement with Global Sale Wholesale could have substantial implications."

My expression solemn as I emphasized the importance of the situation. Dialing Rebeccah's number. The phone rang, and Rebeccah's familiar voice greeted me on the other end.

"Hey, Holli, what's going on?" Her tone laced with curiosity.

"Rebeccah," I began, my focus unwavering, "we have a meeting at my office at 2 p.m. I need you, Samantha, and Breanna there. Justin will join us."

A brief pause followed before Rebeccah responded, her tone reflecting understanding. "Got it, Holli. We'll be there. This sounds significant."

"It is. Thank you, Rebeccah." I ended the call and turned my attention back to my brother.

"I'll grab you a to-go mug," I declared. "Our catch-up time will have to wait – it's time to clear your name."

"Sounds good," Steve agreed, his resolve evident. "I'll get the mug. You freshen up. I guess today is 'bring your brother to work day!'" His laughter filled the room, a moment of lightness amid the gravity of our mission.

"It is," I affirmed with a smile, heading into my room, ready to prepare for the crucial meeting.

Amid the city's pulse, an old familiar tune burst forth from the car's radio. Like a cherished memory, the melody enveloped us in nostalgia and warmth. Steve and I exchanged a knowing glance, our eyes sparkling with shared history. We both surrendered to the music without hesitation, our voices merging in a harmonious duet.

Laughter joined the song and the distant city sounds, carried by the wind streaming through the open windows. Our voices soared with the music, encapsulating a timeless bond that transcended years. The cityscape outside blurred into a tapestry of colors and shapes, our focus fixed on this shared experience. Lyrics became a bridge to cherished memories, a testament to our enduring love.

We reached our destination, and the car stopped in a designated parking spot. The engine's gentle hum ceased, and silence lingered – a pause before the next chapter of our day. Stepping out of the vehicle, a gust of wind brushed against us.

The urban landscape outside stood in contrast to the sleek interior of Winston & Associates. Guiding Steve through the reception area, I led the way with assured strides. Familiar faces and the rhythm of office life greeted us, and Steve's presence radiated warmth and charisma, eliciting smiles from those we passed.

Approaching the reception desk, I introduced my brother to the receptionist. "This is my brother, Steve Bachman," I said, my voice tinged with affection. "Steve, this is Sarah, our wonderful receptionist."

Sarah greeted us with a friendly smile and extended her hand. "It's
a pleasure."

Steve's handshake exuded genuine warmth. "The pleasure is mine,
Sarah. Thank you for having me here."

Upon arriving at my floor, familiarity embraced us. Navigating
the well-known hallway, I exchanged greetings with colleagues and
acquaintances. These interactions showcased my reputation and my
brother's natural charm, making our progress through the office feel
like a warm reunion.

"Welcome to my domain," I greeted with a smile, inviting Steve
to enter. "Make yourself comfortable. Would you like something to
drink?"

"You've made this place your own, Holli. A cup of coffee would be
wonderful, thank you."

Heading to the coffee station in the breakroom, preparing a cup for
Steve as the aroma of brewed coffee filled the air. Returning, I handed
him the cup.

"Thank you," Steve expressed his gratitude.

I glanced at the package sitting on my desk, a sense of anticipation coursing through me. It was Daniel's report, the culmination of
meticulous forensic accounting work that we had been waiting for.
The envelope held the key to clearing Steve's name and uncovering the
truth behind the allegations.

Beside me, Steve's expression mirrored my mixture of excitement
and apprehension. We opened the package together, revealing the
bound report within. Its pages were a treasure trove of information,
organized and presented. I could see Daniel's dedication to detail reflected in every line.

We pored over the report, a whirlwind of emotions swept through us. The data, charts, and analyses sprawled across the pages breathed life into the intricate network of transactions. Each section hinted at a path to redemption, illustrating that Steve's work had adhered to ethical standards and best practices.

The emails he sent contained clear evidence, supported by whistle-blower testimony, that his name had been forged on all financial documents to shield William and Jeff from implication. A wave of relief washed over me. It was evident—my brother had no part in the corruption. He'd stepped away from the position just in time, steering clear of any involvement in the unethical conduct.

"Steve," I began, "This is it. This report is our turning point. We proved your innocence. You will not have to worry about the bar or any ethics investigation."

Steve nodded, his eyes fixed on the pages before us. "Holli, I can't thank you enough for taking on this fight with me. Seeing this report, it's like a weight is lifted." Steve leaned back in his chair, a mix of relief and gratitude washing over him. "Samantha's emails are a testament to the truth. It's clear that everything was above reproach, despite the allegations."

We continued to comb through the report, discussing its implications and brainstorming our next steps. The atmosphere in the room shifted from uncertainty to a shared sense of purpose. With each page we turned, a path illuminated, guiding us toward the resolution we sought.

"Holli," Steve said, "I can't believe how lucky I am to have you in my corner. You've assembled an incredible team, and I'm grateful."

I hugged my brother, "We are family, and this is what family does for each other."

At that moment, a soft knock was at the door. It was Rebeccah, Breanna, and Samantha in time.

"Steve, I'd like to introduce you to my incredible friends," I said with a smile, gesturing toward each of them. "This is Rebeccah, who kickstarted this investigation."

Rebeccah's eyes sparkled with pride and mischief as she extended her hand. "It's a pleasure to meet you. Holli been singing your praises non-stop."

My look shifted to Breanna, whose aura of professionalism was undeniable. "This is Breanna, an investigative reporter for KBNW in Sunnyville. She's a master at uncovering hidden stories and unearthing the facts."

"It's an honor," Breanna said, shaking his hand.

My eyes landed on Samantha, the enigmatic secret weapon of our team. "We have Samantha. She can retrieve information from any-where."

Samantha's smile was mysterious and reassuring as she extended her hand to Steve. "A pleasure, Steve. I promise you, I have a few tricks that might surprise you."

Steve's eyebrows lifted in playful curiosity as he shook Samantha's hand. "I'm intrigued, Samantha. Looking forward to seeing your skills in action."

Laughter filled the room, and our shared understanding created an unbreakable bond.

"All right, everyone," I began, my voice unwavering. "There's some-thing crucial I must share. Steve and I examined Daniel's report, revealing that forensic accounting proves Steve's unwavering ethical stance within Global Sale Wholesale. His involvement poses no hin-drance as we expose Jeff and William. With concrete evidence, we're prepared to bring this matter to court if needed.

"I appreciate each of you," Steve expressed, a mixture of gratitude and relief evident in his words. "Now, I can return home assured that my little sister managed the situation. Samantha, a heartfelt thank you for your exceptional contribution. Holli made it clear, no inquiries about the source or method of obtaining the information," he added with a playful smile, prompting laughter to fill the room.

Just then, Justin knocked on the door. "Good afternoon," he greeted, his voice composed. "I don't believe I have had the pleasure of meeting all of you."

A slight pang of regret tugged at my conscience, and I interjected, "I'm so sorry. Allow me to introduce you." I turned to my friends and introduced them, a sense of pride swelling within me. "These are my dear friends investigating EthicalEdge Solutions and Global Sale Wholesale and their CEOs.

Rebeccah leaned in, her voice steady and focused. "We have evidence that incriminates William Donavan. We have also amassed substantial evidence against Jeff Paulson. Our findings include damning emails, bank statements, and thorough vendor due diligence. They all point to Paulson's involvement in kickbacks."

Justin's expression shifted, and a hint of regret tinged his words. "My legal team advised me to sever any ties that could be traced to any unethical behavior." His look turned toward me, a contemplative look in his eyes. "Holli, I believe it's time to consider a strategic pivot. I recommend severing ties with both EthicalEdge Solutions and Global Sale Wholesale. Your expertise in contract law could prove invaluable in navigating this process. We must extricate ourselves from these partnerships. I have also talked with others. They will begin to sever ties as well."

Nodding with conviction, my resolve unwavering, I said, "I will examine the contracts, strategize the most effective disengagement, and work to ensure our actions align with legal standards. Our primary goal is to achieve clarity while minimizing potential fallout."

A surge of relief washed over Justin's features as I offered. "Come back here tomorrow, and I will draw up the paperwork for your signature," I suggested, my voice carrying a reassuring undertone.

His response was swift and enthusiastic, a glimmer of gratitude in his eyes. "Perfect! 11 AM?" he inquired, seeking confirmation.

Meeting his eyes with a confident nod, sealing our agreement. The weight of uncertainty lifted, replaced by a newfound sense of purpose.

Our meeting with Justin ended, the women gathered their belongings and exchanged smiles. Exiting my office, we walked down the hallway together, our footsteps echoing against the polished floors. We radiated a mix of contentment and anticipation for what lay ahead. Breanna and Rebeccah headed towards the elevators, their voices filled with animated chatter about our next steps. True to her enigmatic nature, Samantha gave us a knowing smile before disappearing down the corridor, her steps purposeful yet shrouded in mystery.

After bidding farewell to my friends, I returned to my office to gather my things. Leaving the office and reaching my car, I found Steve waiting, his expression a mix of curiosity and relief. We drove through the city streets on our way home, the fading sunlight painted everything in a soft, golden hue. The buildings and landmarks we passed by were familiar yet held renewed significance.

A sense of accomplishment washed over us as we pulled into the driveway. Steve and I exited the car, the front porch light flickered to life. Together, we walked towards the entrance, the door opening to reveal the inviting embrace of my home.

"I should head home," Steve mentioned, his tone hinting at reluctance.

"Of course, but remember, you're always welcome here." I nodded, understanding his need to depart yet feeling a twinge of sadness at the prospect of his leaving.

A small smile tugged at the corners of his lips. "I know, stay in touch."

He walked towards his car, and I stood on the porch, watching as he settled into the driver's seat. The engine hummed to life. I waved at him, a gesture filled with fondness and gratitude. Our journey together had brought us closer, and the bonds of family and friendship felt more vital than ever.

Chapter 11

Back at the office the next day, the gentle hum of the air conditioning and the soft rustling of paper created a soothing backdrop, a comforting cadence to my thoughts. I stood by the window, my gaze fixed on the bustling city streets below. A swirl of emotions churned within me. My brother was free from accusations. A joy riveted my heart as he didn't have to face these challenges.

Returning to my desk, I immersed myself in the task at hand. The forms and letters sprawled out before me, promising Justin's liberation from unethical practices. Each stroke of my pen felt deliberate. With meticulous care, I crafted the documents severing Justin's contractual ties with EthicalEdge Solutions and Global Sale Wholesale

At 11 a.m., a familiar knock resonated through my office, punctuating the air with purpose. Rising from my chair and approaching the door, my heart quickened with anticipation and relief. The rhythm of my heartbeat echoed the clock's ticking. I reached for the doorknob, and I swung the door open to reveal Justin's formidable presence.

Immaculate in appearance, his athletic frame exuded a quiet confidence. "Holli," he greeted, his voice steady and appreciative.

Stepping into the conference room, Justin and I took our seats, facing each other across the arranged table. We exchanged a silent understanding. I cleared my throat, ready to begin a significant conversation. I addressed him with professionalism.

"Thank you for being here today. Our objective is to disentangle your charitable endeavors from EthicalEdge Solutions and Global Sale Wholesale," I commented.

Justin's gaze met mine. "Thank you so much."

My response was accompanied by a nod of agreement: "I have prepared the legal documentation for the termination of the contracts. It is outlined in a comprehensive plan."

I explained the specifics of the contract termination process, laying out the timeline for notifying involved parties, the transfer of assets, and the handover of responsibilities, addressing every detail.

As our discussion progressed, Justin's appreciation for my thoroughness became evident. "Holli, your attention to detail is remarkable. You've accounted for every possible angle."

A genuine smile graced my lips, reflecting my unwavering commitment to a seamless and ethical transition. "My foremost priority is safeguarding the integrity of your philanthropic endeavors and ensuring they continue."

Justin and I reviewed and affixed our signatures to the legal documents. Each pen stroke dissolved the contractual duties binding Justin's companies to EthicalEdge Solutions and Global Sale Wholesale. A palpable sense of accomplishment and relief filled the air, like a gentle exhale after a long, challenging journey.

"Thank you, Holli," Justin conveyed genuine and heartfelt gratitude.

A nod of agreement emphasized my understanding. The meeting drew close, and Justin and I rose from our seats. After concluding the meeting with Justin, I took a moment to collect my thoughts. The weight of the discussion lingered in the air, a reminder of the importance of upholding ethical principles in all endeavors. I gathered and organized the documents with a determined exhale, ensuring every detail was in place.

A gentle knock on the office door diverted my focus. Turning towards the sound, I saw the familiar faces of my three friends—Rebeccah, Samantha, and Breanna—standing at the threshold.

"Hey, Holli," Rebeccah began, her voice steady and unwavering. "We've got some crucial information to share with you. Mind if we come in?"

"Of course, come on in," I replied, motioning for them to take a seat.

"After we left last evening," Rebeccah started, her voice tinged with contemplation, "A package was placed at my doorstep. I called Breanna and Samantha. I didn't wish to disturb you or your brother."

"Thank you," I said. "So, what was inside?"

Rebeccah's eyes held a mix of seriousness and concern as she delved into the contents of the package. She began, her voice measured, "several documents, financial records, and correspondence which suggests a troubling pattern. It confirmed Jeff engaged in under-the-table transactions and economic agreements with some of the suppliers we've been working with."

Breanna chimed in, her facial expression a blend of shock and anger. "Yes, and the documents indicate William and Jeff were receiving substantial kickbacks from suppliers in exchange for awarding them contracts and ensuring their continued partnership."

Samantha's voice carried a hint of disbelief. "It's disturbing to see how long this corruption went. The evidence suggests that Jeff exploited his position for personal gain for quite some time."

My mind racing to process the gravity of the situation. "Do the documents provide a clear trail of transactions?"

Nodding, Samantha said, "Indeed, they do. There's a paper trail linking payments from suppliers to shell companies of Paulson. It's a sophisticated scheme, but the proof is quite compelling."

Rebeccah's heart sank as she realized her company's misconduct. " Not only was Jeff betraying our company's values, but he was also enriching himself at the expense of our integrity and mission."

Samantha's eyes met mine, her resolve matching my own. "We're prepared to take the documentation to the proper channels and expose William and Jeff's actions."

Rebeccah's look turned resolute as she leaned forward, her voice expressing urgency. "At the board meeting tomorrow, I'm going before the board to give them the proof we've uncovered."

Samantha held a note of approval. "Rebeccah, it is a courageous step to take."

"Did the package contain anything else? Perhaps something could establish a connection between William and the Child Labor Laws violations?" I inquired.

"Yes," Breanna began, "We found these documents inside the package. They lay out a series of transactions between Global Sale Wholesale and a shell company."

With the evidence against William and his connection to the exploitative practices becoming undeniable. The four of us knew it was time to take our findings to the authorities.

Pooling our strengths, we collaborated seamlessly to craft a compelling report. The process unfolded, and before we knew it, the task was complete. Fatigue tugged at our edges, a testament to the hours of relentless effort we had poured into this endeavor.

Breanna leaned forward, her expression intense. "Everything is in order. Let's go and speak with my contacts at the police station. We'll ensure the evidence is in the hands of those we can trust to investigate."

Breanna's voice shifted, a note of deliberation entering her tone. "You know," she began, "I know someone who will greatly benefit this case. I have worked with him on several news stories, and he has quite a reputation, Detective John Knox. I think requesting him for this case might be advantageous." Her words hung in the air, sparking a moment of contemplative silence.

Breanna's gaze met Rebeccah's as she continued, "He is helpful and known for his thoroughness and dedication. Given the sensitivity and complexity of the evidence we've provided, having someone like him leading the investigation could be a game-changer."

Samantha nodded in agreement. "Breanna's right. Knox has a reputation for being relentless. His involvement could assure us our findings won't be overlooked or swept under the rug."

My lips curled into a thoughtful smile. "All right, let's do it. I'll contact the precinct and request him."

We stepped into the bustling precinct, and the familiar aura of law enforcement enveloped us. The rhythmic clatter of computer keyboards and the hushed conversations of officers punctuated the air. The four of us exchanged determined glances, our resolve unwavering as we approached the front desk.

Rebeccah cleared her throat and addressed the officer behind the desk. "We're here to see Detective Knox. Is he available?"

The officer regarded us with a professional expression before picking up the phone and making a brief call. After a moment, he gestured for us to sit in the waiting area adjacent to the front desk. We complied, our anticipation growing as we exchanged muted whispers about what lay ahead.

Detective Knox emerged from his office, his gaze falling upon me. Our eyes met, and in a fleeting moment, I sensed something beyond the confines of our shared mission. His deep blue eyes held a warmth and intensity.

It was as if the universe had orchestrated this encounter, weaving a narrative of intrigue and perhaps even more. Caught in the web of his commanding demeanor, I couldn't help but feel a flutter of nerves as I managed to stammer, "Hello." My greeting carried a hint of vulnerability, betraying a touch of awe his presence evoked.

"Good evening, ladies," he greeted us with a nod, looking straight at me. His gaze lingered, and a small smile formed. His voice was measured, carrying a hint of intrigue. "I understand you're here to speak with me?"

Rebeccah, always the one to take the lead, stood and extended her hand. "Yes. Thank you for seeing us. I'm Rebeccah, and these are my friends Holli, Breanna, and Samantha."

Detective Knox shook Rebeccah's hand before focusing on the rest of us. "A pleasure to meet you all. Please follow me to my office."

Aware of the sidelong glances and subtle nods passing among the officers. Whispers fluttered like secretive confidences exchanged in the corridors. His office reflected his personality—organized and arranged. He motioned for us to sit, his gaze resting on the report we had brought with us. "I understand you have some information you'd like to share?"

Rebeccah nodded and explained the report's contents, highlighting the facts compiled and the connections uncovered. He listened. He asked probing questions, delving deeper into the intricacies of the case as he sought to grasp the full scope of our findings.

His scrutiny didn't waver, his questions piercing yet respectful. He leaned back in his chair, studying each of us. "You've done impressive work," he acknowledged with a glint of admiration.

Rebeccah extended the report to him. "We're committed to assisting in any way we can."

He flipped through the pages. "I appreciate your diligence. Paulson has been involved in embezzlement and fraud. Donavan is the worst kind. Your efforts won't go unnoticed." His eyes lingered on me, making me blush.

Seeing the exchange, Samantha chuckled and said, "Well, ladies, it's time to go!"

I couldn't shake the admiration that settled within me. His enigmatic character intrigued me by the layers he guarded beneath his composed exterior.

Breanna, Samantha, and Rebeccah exchanged knowing glances as we walked, their expressions reflecting the unspoken connection Detective Knox and I shared.

"Rebeccah," I announced with a playful smile, "you've got just one task for tonight."

She arched an eyebrow in curiosity. "Oh?"

"Prepare yourself for the ultimate board meeting of your life," I quipped, offering her a wink.

Chapter 12

I still could not shake the thoughts of the brief encounter with Detective Knox. The glances and exchanges replayed in my mind, their significance unfurling like threads of intrigue woven into my thoughts. The memory of his deep blue eyes, a blend of warmth and intensity, lingered like an echo. I needed to concentrate on my work, but these memories made it difficult.

Perusing the files, documents, and contracts across my desk, my thoughts were caught in a delicate balance between the immediate tasks and tonight's meeting. A soft knock on my office door shattered the reverie that had enveloped me. Rebeccah's presence was a welcome interruption. She embodied purpose as she exuded a palpable aura of resolve. Clad in a pristine suit and radiating confidence, she wore her hair pulled back in an unpretentious yet polished style.

Rebeccah and I left my office. We arrived at EthicalEdge Solutions, where the familiar figures of Breanna and Samantha were waiting. Breanna stood adorned in a sleek ivory dress, underscoring her authoritative demeanor. Her hair was sculpted into a polished updo, and her frame accentuated her features and projected an aura of precision.

The determination in her gaze was palpable, a clear indication of her readiness to unravel the intricacies awaited. Beside Breanna, Samantha wore a tailored emerald green dress that resonated with her lively spirit. Her hair, a cascade of luxuriant blonde waves, cascaded around her face in an effortless display of grace. The intensity in her eyes mirrored her unwavering commitment, a testament to her dedication to the task.

We approached the elevator together, the soft chime signaling their ascent to the uppermost floor. The doors opened, and we stepped out onto the polished corridor, the subtle click of our heels a synchronized cadence of purpose. The path ahead led to the imposing entrance of the boardroom, a threshold marked the juncture where our collective determination and resolve would soon converge.

The boardroom door swung open with a sense of gravitas, revealing an expanse of polished wood and high-backed chairs arranged around a long, imposing table. Soft, muted light cascaded from elegant chandeliers overhead.

Emotions swirled in the air – a mix of nervous energy, steely resolve, and the weight of responsibility. The board meeting was geared up, and the room was filled with men in suits, including Jeff Paulson, the CEO of EthicalEdge Solutions. His smug demeanor hinted at his ignorance, not knowing what was coming his way. I nudged Rebeccah, catching her attention and directing it toward Jeff.

"It's happening," Rebeccah sighed.

"Are we in the 'New Business' portion?" I asked.

"Yeah, I scheduled us in when we started digging," she confirmed.

The meeting progressed toward the 'New Business' portion, the moment for unveiling the truth about the company's operations and

Jeff Paulson's actions. Rebeccah was poised, ready for the confrontation.

"Any new business to discuss?" The chairman's voice rang out, cutting through the room. Rebeccah took a deep breath, and the room fell silent. "Members of the board," Rebeccah's voice resonated with authority and conviction, "Prepare for a comprehensive account of our organization's unethical practices. We must illuminate the actions of one individual who betrayed this company's and its stakeholders' trust."

Breanna's contribution echoed the gravity of her findings. "Concrete evidence from eyewitnesses and whistle-blowers reveals a pattern of deception, from embezzlement to fraudulent transactions. Jeff Paulson's actions compromised financial integrity and tarnished the reputation of EthicalEdge Solutions. The partnership established with Global Sale Wholesale and William Donovan involved exploiting children overseas in abhorrent working conditions and extended hours."

Samantha's words cut through the tension, her voice decisive. "The plan was to profit from selling lines of clothes, siphon money off the top, and conceal it in shell companies worldwide. Witnesses, whistle-blowers, and emails have confirmed this elaborate scheme."

"Jeff Paulson and William Donavan have remained undetected with customs, their names absent from any of the accounting. Their head of accounting even forged their attorney's name to be implicated." I said, looking right at Jeff. "Adding to the gravity, Justin Ford of the Emerald City Thunderhawks severed ties today with EthicalEdge Solutions due to the partnership with Global Sale Wholesale, and other athletes will likely join him," I declared.

Jeff's smug facade crumbled into anxiety, his eyes darting around, searching for an escape route. The room succumbed to a heavy silence as our words reverberated, exposing a depth of corruption extending beyond financial wrongdoing.

Rebeccah's calm assertion cut through the tension. "I enjoyed working for you, Jeff, but William left you hanging. Local authorities have been informed. Get yourself an attorney; you'll need one. Looking at the board's chairman, she declared, "It's our collective responsibility to take swift and decisive action. Jeff's actions have harmed this company, perpetuating a cycle of wrongdoing. I call for an immediate termination of Jeff Paulson as CEO of EthicalEdge Solutions."

Jeff exited as fast as he could not staying for the vote or the results.

Rebeccah delivered the rest of the presentation in the boardroom, where the atmosphere was thick with tension. The board members expressed shock and disbelief as she exposed Jeff's deceitful web of financial misconduct.

Rebeccah concluded her presentation, and a charged energy filled the room—outrage. "Thank you for bringing this to our attention," the chairman spoke, his voice carrying a weight mirroring the seriousness of the situation. We will review the evidence presented and act accordingly."

The corridor outside the boardroom reflected the positive energy. The soft echoes of our footsteps marked the transition from the boardroom to the outside world, a world that now held the promise of positive change. We approached our respective cars outside the building. We were a quartet of empowered women embarking on the next chapter of our journey.

The car engines hummed to life, and headlights pierced the darkness as we formed a small convoy, a visual testament to the unity which had propelled us forward. Rebeccah and I were in the lead car. Our conversation flowed. We reflected on the board meeting, our words infused with a sense of achievement. Rebeccah's excitement was palpable as she recounted moments, her voice carrying pride and determination.

In the second car, Breanna and Samantha engaged in a spirited dialogue, their voices rising and falling like a harmonious melody. Their friendship was evident in how they bounced ideas off each other, a testament to their cultivated synergy.

Through the windows, creating a backdrop of urban beauty mirrored the dynamic energy within the cars. The passing scenes blended seamlessly with the discussions.

The convoy pulled into my driveway, the engines stopping. We stepped out of our cars, our voices and laughter still echoing our vibrant discussions. A testament to the genuine friendship that bound us together. The night was young, setting the stage for a celebration that would mark our achievements, and the unbreakable bond of friendship had brought us together.

Epilogue

A few months have slipped by since the pivotal night in the boardroom, and the echoes of our collective efforts still reverberate within me. The aftermath was swift – Jeff Paulson, stripped of his authority, was ushered out of the company's corridors with a heavy cloak of disgrace. I couldn't help but have a pang of sympathy, a fleeting emotion mingled with the unwavering satisfaction of justice served.

Detective Knox, in collaboration with a counterpart from the local FBI field office, intensified their efforts, directing their attention towards unraveling the intricate web woven by William Donavan and his elusive network of shell companies. The Department of Homeland Security joined the pursuit, a formidable force set on bringing justice to those who exploited child labor.

The pursuit of Dillian Turner, a shadowy figure lurking at the edges of our quest, intensified. Rumors whispered of William's and Dillian's confinement in a foreign prison, the wheels of justice turning as extradition proceedings sought to return them to our shores.

A celebratory buzz filled the air as I stood in my backyard, surrounded by friends. Sizzling burgers on the grill mingled with the crisp evening breeze, creating an inviting atmosphere of togetherness and joy. The sky hues of orange and pink as the sun dipped below the horizon, casting a serene glow over the scene.

Laughter and chatter echoed around me, each voice a note in the symphony of friendship which brought us together. The clinking of glasses and the occasional burst of joy added a musical rhythm to the backdrop of our celebration. The gentle rustle of leaves in the trees joined the chorus, creating a harmonious blend of nature and human interaction.

Justin, with his vibrant energy, stood by the grill. The aroma of grilled meat wafted through the air, accompanied by the irresistible sizzle, promising a delectable feast. His smile was infectious, and beside him was April, whose presence radiated happiness and contentment. Their connection was evident in how they exchanged glances, a silent language that spoke volumes about a growing love between them.

The construction of Justin's football stadium loomed in the background. This was a testament to his dreams taking shape, and ready to welcome fans in the upcoming season. In my heart, I held a wish for their happiness, a silent hope their journey together would reflect love and fulfillment.

My brother, a beacon of rekindled kinship, stood nearby. The bonds that had laid dormant for too long and the warmth of our connection enveloped me. His presence was a reminder of the time lost, now replaced with a growing bond that held the promise of shared memories and newfound closeness. The sounds of his laughter mingled with those around us, a testament to the joy his company brought into my life. Our meetings became regular, and his visits to my home, now a cherished tradition, filling my heart with gratitude.

Knox, having another side to the stoicism, also had a good-hearted nature and operated the grill. His skillful hands flipped burgers, a culinary maestro orchestrating a symphony of flavors. His sense of humor and easygoing demeanor were a perfect match for the light-hearted atmosphere of our gathering. Humor flowed between us, reflecting our comfort in each other's company. He had been a pleasant surprise, a reminder life's unexpected turns led to the most beautiful connections. I found myself enamored and anticipated the endless possibilities for us.

Samantha, a genius in her own right, added an air of intrigue to the mix. Her ability to navigate digital realms was awe-inspiring, and we still did not inquire too much into the origins of her information. Her mind was a treasure trove of knowledge; her humor keeps us laughing. She continues to be a friend we were fortunate to have. We still have no idea who she works for or what she does, but it will remain a mystery.

Breanna's was a testament to the power of unwavering dedication. Her career skyrocketed with the removal of Jeff Paulson, and the subsequent investigation which exposed William Donavan's web of deception. The accolades followed, culminating in a prestigious Emmy Award nomination for her impactful reporting. Her tenacity and passion set her on a trajectory of success. She had many offers for a promotion, and she chose a smaller market in a town called Centerville, about two hours away.

Rebeccah, the unexpected bond blossomed from a chance encounter at a fundraiser. Her friendship was a beacon of light in my life, a kindred spirit whose company enriched my journey in ways I never anticipated. Her recent promotion to Chief Marketing Officer was a testament to her skills and dedication, a role convincing Justin to return to EthicalEdge Solutions.

Her unwavering support and genuine friendship were gifts I held close to my heart. Amidst the gathered crowd, Rebeccah stood as a beacon of warmth and camaraderie. Her impact, a steady anchor around which our circle formed. She lifted her glass, a sense of unity enveloped us, a shared purpose transcending boundaries.

"To love and friendship," her voice rang out, the words carrying a weight resonated deep within. The sentiment echoed through the air, a chorus of affirmation connected us all. The glasses clinked, a symphony of celebration reverberating through the space.

Laughter, delicate and effervescent, followed the toast. It bubbled forth like a clear stream, carrying the essence of joy and shared merriment. Each peal of chuckling was a brushstroke on the canvas of the evening, painting a portrait of happiness adorned the atmosphere.

I stood there, surrounded by the laughter, the connections, and the sense of purpose that defined this moment. I couldn't help but marvel at the transformative journey of the past four months. The metamorphosis from a work-focused attorney to a friend who embraced life's adventures had been profound. The path ahead was uncertain, but with these three friends by my side, I knew it held the promise of joy, growth, and shared experiences only true friendships could unveil.

Acknowledgements

Creating a book transcends the solitary act of typing on an author's keyboard. It's a collaborative effort involving numerous individuals, each contributing to the tapestry that brings forth the mesmerizing worlds an author unveils. This book stands as a testament to that collective endeavor. Behind its pages lies a dedicated and talented team fervently weaving together a narrative brimming with strength, transformation, and the enduring bonds of friendship. To my wife Holli, who helped edit this book, your guidance, and unwavering support have been instrumental in shaping this story, infusing it with depth and clarity. A heartfelt appreciation extends to my cover artist, Sadia Asif. Your creative vision has given this tale its visual essence, breathing life onto its cover and beyond. Yet, paramount among my acknowledgments is to my beloved family. To my wife, Holli, and daughters, Breanna, Rebeccah, and Samantha—you are the heartbeat of my inspiration. Your unwavering love and encouragement have been the guiding light throughout this journey. I cherish you all deeply. – John Russell

Bonus Material—Investigation Series Book 2—

HEROES OF CENTERVILLE

The soft morning sunlight filtered through the curtains, casting a warm and gentle glow across the room. I blinked, remnants of sleep slowly giving way to a new day. Stretching beneath the comfort of my sheets, the air felt fresh and invigorating, with a hint of dew and the promise of a new beginning.

Centerville, California, welcomed me with quiet serenity, unlike any place I had lived. The view from my window painted a picturesque scene—the gentle swaying of tall trees, their leaves whispering secrets to the breeze; the distant silhouette of neighboring houses, each with its own story to tell; and a sliver of the clear blue sky, promising a day of possibilities.

The sounds of morning began to fill the air—a distant chirping of birds as they greeted the day, the occasional soft rustling of leaves as a squirrel scurried along a branch, and the gentle hum of a passing car in the distance. Each sound carried a sense of familiarity, welcoming me to this new chapter of my life.

My decision to move to Centerville marked a turning point in my life. Months of contemplation led me to this choice, a deliberate evaluation of the merits and drawbacks of various towns and cities. After years of relentless investigative journalism culminated in receiving an Emmy award for a high-profile exposé. I yearned for change. The unrelenting pursuit of truth had exacted its toll, leaving me with a deep longing for a place to rediscover solace and replenish my spirit.

Centerville had entered my consciousness almost serendipitously, a small town with warmth and friendliness. Its picturesque charm and tight-knit community beckoned me, offering a sanctuary far removed from the frantic pace of the city. The decision to uproot my life was not devoid of challenges and uncertainties.

Swinging my legs over the edge of the bed, my feet met the cool hardwood floor, sending a gentle shiver up my spine. Catching myself in the mirror, the vibrant hue of my auburn hair caught the light, creating a warm halo that seemed to dance with every step. My brown eyes, deep and determined, held an intense curiosity, always seeking the hidden truths beneath the surface.

The teapot whistle eased my tension, and the scent of freshly brewed tea wafted in from the kitchen, a comforting aroma that instantly eased any residual grogginess. It mingled with the faint smell of cardboard and packing tape, a reminder that boxes were still waiting to go through.

Walking across the room, I opened the window, inviting the crisp morning air to fill the space. It carried the faint perfume of blooming flowers, a testament to the vibrant nature surrounding my apartment. A gentle breeze danced through the room, ruffling the curtains and bringing a sense of renewal.

Excitement and apprehension filled me as I focused on the boxes lining the walls. Each box held a piece of my past, a collection of memories and possessions that would soon find their place in this new space. Though slightly overwhelming, the sight of the boxes filled me with a sense of purpose—a reminder that this was a fresh start, a chance to create a unique living space.

I began unpacking, and the room gradually transformed from a sea of cardboard into a haven of familiarity. The soft clink of dishes placed on shelves, the satisfying thud of books finding their home on a shelf, and the gentle rustling of linens spread over the bed—it was a symphony of settling in. This melody played out against the backdrop of a new beginning.

The air filled with quiet anticipation, nostalgia, and accomplishment. I carefully unwrapped the well-padded box that held the precious treasure—a gleaming Emmy award that was a testament to years of hard work and dedication. The morning sun's reflection on the golden surface mirrored the satisfaction glow from within.

The memory of that pivotal investigation at KBNW played like a filmstrip. The relentless pursuit of uncovering the story of Jeff Paulson and the web of kickbacks he had orchestrated during his tenure as CEO of Ethical Edge Solutions, and William Donavan and the unethical child labor practices of Global Sale Wholsellers. Late nights poring over documents, daring interviews with insiders, and heart-pounding moments of unveiling the shocking truth flooded back, filling the room with a sense of accomplishment that words could hardly capture.

Placing the Emmy on a shelf, its presence infused the room with recognition and honor. The muted clink of metal against wood resonated with a sense of validation—a culmination of years of dedication to my investigative reporting. The award stood not only as a personal achievement but also as a tribute to the power of journalism to uncover injustice and spark change.

Next to the Emmy, I reached for a framed photograph nestled among the unpacked items. A snapshot was taken during the celebration BBQ following the successful airing of the Jeff Paulson & William Donavan investigation. In the photo, I stood alongside my dear friends—Holli, Rebeccah, and Samantha. Our smiles were broad, our eyes alight with a shared sense of triumph and friendship. I felt warmth and gratitude as I looked at the photograph. These women had been my pillars of support, my confidantes through the challenges and victories of my career. The laughter, the late-night discussions, and the unwavering encouragement were all encapsulated in that single frame. It was a tangible reminder that I was never alone on this journey; the success I celebrated reflected the bonds we had forged and the strength of our friendship.

Gently tracing my fingers over the photograph's glass, memories cascaded like a waterfall. The camaraderie captured in that frozen photo transcended the glossy surface—an unspoken pact forged in shared dreams and unbreakable connections. As sunlight danced on the photograph, I couldn't help but smile, recognizing various experiences leading me to this moment. We unraveled the intricate web of the kickback scheme, emotions surging through me like a storm. Each friend brought a unique strength to our collective quest for justice. Their unwavering support and shared determination filled me with a profound sense of unity and purpose. In the face of adversity, their friendship was a light guiding us through the challenges ahead.

The move to Centerville had been a daring venture into the unknown. Leaving behind the comfort of familiarity, I embraced the challenge of weaving my story into the fabric of a new community. Centerville's quaint streets and rich history welcomed me. This town became my fresh start, a new chapter in my narrative. The Emmy is a symbol of triumph, illuminating new paths. Its presence opened doors to unexpected opportunities. Now, the station in Centerville extended an invitation to become the morning anchor—a crucial step towards broader aspirations.

Another thought emerged as I weighed the gravity of the morning anchor position. Amidst the task at hand, a yearning to explore the uncharted began to take shape, an itch to immerse myself in the unfamiliar of this new town. The notion of a farmer's market, a vibrant hub of local life, beckoned to me like a siren's call. It held the key to unraveling the essence of this place—an opportunity to connect, learn, and paint my strokes on the canvas of Centerville's narrative.

Determined, I set the boxes aside, ready to venture beyond my doorstep into the vibrant world outside. The journey to the farmer's market engulfed me in a whirlwind of sensations. Colorful produce stalls, artisans crafting their wares, and people from all walks of life converged in a lively dance of activity, forming a vivid tapestry before my eyes.